MARKED AT MIDNIGHT

MARK OF THE DRAGON, BOOK 1

CLAIRE CONRAD

MARKED AT MIDNIGHT

MARK OF THE DRAGON, BOOK 1

An ordinary night.
An ordinary bar.
Two extraordinary men.

When the nearly identical hunks of male perfection walk into the restaurant where Brittany works, she absolutely, positively does not expect them to glance her way.

They don't just glance, they stare.

She does not expect a proposition so hot she can barely believe it. Still, she accepts. Eagerly.

And one night of passion ruins her for every other man on the planet.
She can't stop thinking about them.
Wanting them.
Needing them.

But they aren't what they seem.
They're not human, but Dragon and Rider.

Beast and Dragonborn.

They live to protect humanity. To protect life.

But war is brewing...
dragon vs dragon,
brother vs brother,
ice vs fire.

Brittany soon finds herself not just giving them her heart,
but in the middle of a war she can't possibly understand.
And her love is the key to not only her survival but theirs.
To the survival of the entire world.

CHAPTER 1

Brittany Anderson, Chicago, Illinois

WITH A SIGH OF RELIEF, I pulled into the parking lot of *Dave's Tavern*. The neon sign was beginning to short, obviously on the edge of going out, the *D* and *T* already having given up. From a distance, it said *ave's avern*.

The bar and restaurant was located in an old dock warehouse with the expected rustic look all the way through. Dave had wanted it to be natural, comfortable, and homey throughout. There were wooden picnic tables for the booths and horseshoes decorating the walls. Had I not worked for the place, it wouldn't have been my first choice for dinner, but it was more home than my crappy apartment and I hadn't had lunch. Or breakfast. And Dave almost always let me eat for free.

As I parked my car, surrounded by several others, I felt a bit

1

more relaxed. It was a relief to be around other people, this probably being the first time I was excited to see a couple smoking outside. Everything seemed normal, peaceful—safe. I needed the security of other people after my strange trip to the park.

Walking in, I made my way through the people standing around and slid onto a bar stool. I smiled as the bartender, a good friend and boss, made his way over. "Hey, Dave."

"There's my girl. You hungry?" Dave was old enough to be my father, and he acted like one, watching all the action going on in the bar every night, and making sure the worst of the assholes found the door.

"Starving. Can I get a burger, fries, a beer and a shot of Tequila?"

His brows rose, but he placed a shot glass on the wooden bar and filled it with his best Tequila before grabbing a slice of lime and placing it on a fresh napkin. "That bad, huh?"

I reached for the salt and let the alcohol burn away the lingering chill from the parking lot. "Not great." I had the lime in my mouth when the other bartender, Pete, came over to eavesdrop.

Pete had dropped out of college the year before and was pursuing a music career. While not many people agreed with that choice, I understood it. The man had talent and the looks to go along with it. He had tattoos on every inch of arm you could see and a tall, thin frame. He had no trouble attracting the ladies. He'd probably slept with every single woman who worked here, all of them but me.

"When you going to come back to work, Brittany? The new

girls are clumsy and make my job a *lot* harder." He leaned against the bar and smiled at me.

I shrugged and continued to smile. "Hey, I earned this vacation." I had enough money saved to take off at least a month. I wanted a chance to get to know my brother. Maybe take a road trip or two. Think about what I was going to do with the rest of my life.

"Yeah? Well, if you get bored, talk to Dave. We need extra help this week."

"Fine." I would help out. I always did. But I had no intention of waiting tables for the rest of my life. The money was usually great, but the back-breaking work wasn't. It was also a real buzzkill to bust ass on a big party then have everyone snub you or leave a two dollar tip on over a hundred dollars' worth of food, dozens of drink refills, and tons of, "Hey, honey, can I get some ketchup?" only to come back with it for someone else at the table to send me off for something else—rinse and repeat for two or three hours.

But that was the job. Sometimes the customers really were friendly and tipped well, and other times they are only nice to get good service and then don't tip—or they were complete jerks and didn't tip regardless. I had no interest in going back just yet, and I was focused on other things anyway. Once I found my brother, my plan was to get a job in an office somewhere. I could answer phones and type at a decent speed. I knew my way around a computer. It wasn't the greatest plan, but I hoped there would be fewer drunken idiots grabbing my ass without an invitation.

Dave placed a mug of my favorite beer down in front of me and frowned. "How much have you saved up, Brittany?"

"Enough, Dave, trust me." I took a big drink from the mug, finally starting to shake off the uneasiness I had felt in the park.

We all talked between their customers as I tore my way through the amazing food and relatively good beer. A hockey game was on one channel and a basketball game on the other. Occasionally, someone in the bar would shout when their team made a good play.

Outside, families and business people sat on the pier overlooking the water, enjoying thick steaks and lobsters dipped in butter. Dave's sign might be on the blink, but business was good. It had always been good. The place was a local hangout, and everyone around knew where the best steaks and seafood could be found.

But in here, in the bar, I was more than content with my burger and beer.

You can take the girl out of the country, but you can't take the country out of the girl.

The mundane noise flowed around me. The longer I sat in the familiar environment, the better I felt. Halfway through my burger, the door opened and I saw two men enter out of the corner of my eye. I felt a change in the air and looked around the bar as every other woman—whether she was engaged in conversation or sitting alone—turned to watch them walk in.

I'd heard the door but hadn't bothered to turn around. But, hell, if they were interesting enough to get the attention of every female in the room, I wanted to see what the big deal was.

I tried not to look at them where they'd notice, but it was difficult. Though, I was pretty sure I wouldn't be noticed any more than the rest of the women in the room.

As I got a good look, I saw what the rest had seen. They had a presence that was magnetic. I felt my womanly parts stir when I looked into the eyes of the first one. Green. Intense. Focused.

Lust. Sex. Desire. They were all in his eyes...and he was looking at me.

When the room started to spin, I realized I had stopped breathing.

I thought this kind of reaction was a myth, something that only happened in romance novels, but I literally could not look away. He held my gaze for a minute and then started to look around the bar like he was searching for someone. That's when I noticed the second one was staring straight at me as well. My nipples were already hard, but my pussy clenched and everything felt heavy, like I should just melt into a puddle right here, right now, and let them do whatever they wanted with me.

I reached for my beer. My hand was shaking so badly it would have sloshed over the top of the chilled mug if it had been full.

Oh, my God, they're twins.

As I sat there, caught in their web, my brain had a hard time wrapping around the fact there were not one, but two of the gorgeous creatures. The only difference I could see in my brief assessment of the two was the one staring me down now was a few inches taller. And their eyes. The first one's eyes had been green, like thick summer grass. This one's eyes were a strangely hypnotic amber, and as he stared, I felt like he was peering into my soul.

Talk about ridiculous romantic nonsense. I had to be more rattled by the creepy episode in the park than I thought.

I'd been savoring the tequila shot, sipping at it, letting it burn on my tongue between bites of my burger. But as I tore my gaze from the amber-eyed sex god and his smoking hot companion, I slammed what was left and closed my eyes hoping the burn would distract my libido from its very dangerous thoughts. Namely me, the moist, creamy filling in a sex god sandwich.

When I opened my eyes, I was paralyzed. He was standing directly in front of me. His scent washed over me like a drug, making me think of wild wind and campfires and man. I'd never smelled anything like it and wondered if it was an outrageously expensive cologne—or just *him.*

My pussy shoved the thoughts right out of my head, screamed right back to the front of the line, blaring at me to take this one home and make him mine. Take him deep. *Surrender.*

What the hell was wrong with me? I didn't have time for this kind of bullshit. I didn't date much, let alone pick up strangers in bars and…

He smiled and my entire body caught on fire. I shifted on the barstool, my dinner long forgotten as I was consumed with lust for the man in front of me. It was an odd reaction.

They were hot, but my reaction to him wasn't like me. Perhaps it had been too long since I'd had sex after all. At that moment, it felt like it had been an eternity. It took all I had to keep from saying something stupid, or worse, *doing* something stupid. Like licking my lips.

Suddenly they were so dry I couldn't seem to stop myself. His gaze followed the motion with a level of attention I'd never had from a man. I wanted him to kiss me. Right there. In front of the whole damn bar. But he didn't move. Just watched me. Made me melt. And squirm. And want.

Finally, after several moments, I found my voice. "Hello." The greeting came in a croak. Of course, a hot man approached me and I channeled my inner frog.

He didn't speak; he continued to stare and tilted his head to look me over. I immediately felt hotter, my body heating up enough I wanted to fan myself like some crazed dog in heat in the middle of summer.

Under his gaze, the heat between my legs turned into a full-fledged vibrating need. I wondered how red my face was now because the heat had moved into my cheeks. There was a thin layer of sweat on my body. He still didn't say anything, probably because he knew what he was. That man was *more* than aware of how beautiful he was, how enraptured he made all the women in his immediate vicinity.

I was a practical woman. I never believed in vampires or werewolves or any of that kind of mystical, magical nonsense. But as loudly as the logical part of my head was screaming that something was *not right,* my body was louder, telling my head to shut the fuck up and let me have what I wanted. Him. No, them. Both of them. I wanted both of them.

The other twin was still walking around the bar. I couldn't figure out if he was looking for some*one* or some*thing.* He looked in booths, at the people sitting in them, despite the strange looks he was getting.

Amber Eye's grin turned into a smile showing perfect teeth. I had a sudden urge to press myself against him. It was a strong desire bordering on a physical *need* and I wrapped my hands around the edge of the bar top to make sure I didn't go anywhere.

What the hell was happening to me? This was insane.

The shorter twin finally returned to his brother and stood right next to him, regarding me with curiosity. I still felt the lust, but it was tampered down a bit with the addition of a new party.

"I'm Zach, this is my brother Iavo. He's mute." The way green eyes said it was so casual, like how he'd say his brother was an architect. I was relieved to know there was a reason Iavo hadn't spoken to me. "He wants to sleep with you; he wants you to sleep with *us*."

Zach moved forward and brushed my cheek with his as he pushed the hair away from my ear. The touch of his skin almost burned against mine. It felt incredible.

My eyes were wide, possibly about to fall out of my head. "I'm sorry?" was the only thing I could think to say as I trembled against the nearness of him, against the heat radiating off his skin. The scent of his skin. He smelled divine. More man, less wild. Pine and heat and sex.

I was going to faint if I didn't start breathing.

Zach's lips brushed against my ear as he whispered in a heated voice, "Come to our cabin. Come play. I promise you won't be disappointed."

The heat moved through my body again, chills moving right alongside. I realized Iavo had moved forward and put his hand on my thigh. The source of all the heat in my body was spreading from his fingers. This thing between us was an undeniable attraction, and even if I'd wanted to play hard to get, I'm not sure that I could have.

"Do you need help, Brittany?" Pete's voice interrupted my momentary departure from reality, and I shook my head quickly. Too quickly. More like a toddler with the big bad adult threatening to take away her candy.

I swallowed hard, knowing if I tried to speak before doing so, it would come out as another embarrassing croak. "No, Pete, but thanks." I wanted this candy all to myself.

The silent one turned to look at the bartender; something almost scary flashed in his amber eyes.

Without hesitation, Zach placed his hand on his brother's shoulder. "Iavo, go sit over there while I talk to the lady." Iavo turned his angry eyes on his brother, but he went over to a corner booth and sat down. I saw one of the women who'd been watching from the other side of the bar make her way over to him.

Turning his attention back to me, Zach quietly said, "If you can't handle two men at once, you need to tell me now." He gently brushed a loose lock of hair back and pinned it behind my ear. "Once we get you in our cabin, there is no turning back."

I should have felt scared, threatened maybe, but excitement pounded through my veins. The feeling that moved through me was too much to resist. I wanted them both, though I'd never been with two men at once. It would be something different for me, but it had been so long since I'd had sex and my body was thrumming with a lot of pent up energy just looking at the twins.

My eyes wandered across the room, and I saw the confident woman was trying to talk to Iavo. She stood next to his table, twirling her hair. She had big breasts, black hair to her waist, and curves to die for, but his eyes hadn't left me. He stared with an intensity that was almost palpable in the room. The tension could be cut with a knife.

Had these two been the ones watching me in the park?

No. No way. That had been frightening. Creepy. This was all heat and lust mixed with excitement. My actions were no longer my own. I was driven by the desire that pooled in my abdomen and the heart beating wildly in my chest.

Iavo continued to stare at me, and the woman finally huffed off, obviously upset by her lack of success.

"I can handle it," I said with more confidence than I felt. I saw Iavo tense at my words, as if he'd actually heard me from across the room. My stomach was flipping again, but it was more out of anticipation than fear.

Zach didn't say anything else. He looked at Iavo who stood and came over to us. I wondered how much of the psychic twin thing they had going on. Especially since Iavo couldn't communicate with sound. It was obvious early on that he didn't use sign language either. So, just how did these two communicate?

Did I care?

No. Not right now I didn't.

Taking my hand, Iavo laced our fingers together and pulled me toward the door. I slid off the bar stool and followed without thinking twice. Zach followed behind and it felt surreal going to two strangers' cabin to give myself to them freely. The women in the bar stared. Some glared as I walked by them. I felt the urge to throw my head back and laugh, swing my hips and flip them off as we left, but I contained the urge. They weren't *mine.* They were just mine for tonight.

The two men were gorgeous in every way, and they wanted

to be with *me*. It was very clear they could have anyone in the bar they wanted, and they'd chosen me. That was exciting, especially when it was obvious all the other women in the room were so jealous.

My brother will still be at the college in the morning, I told myself. I reached my hand into my pocket to feel for the piece of paper. I knew the address by heart from the number of times I'd looked at it, but I kept the scratch paper as a security blanket of sorts. The hope I carried around in that small piece of paper was often my only friend, the one constant in my life, and the key to finding my brother. It had taken me years of research and a lucky break to find him. And all this time, he'd been in the same city, only a few miles away.

Iavo held my hand on the way out of the bar, escorting me until we arrived at a nice black truck. He opened the passenger door for me, and I climbed in, buckling into the middle of the bench seat. Zach climbed into the driver's seat and Iavo into the passenger side next to me. They didn't speak as they buckled in, and I began to worry about *exactly* what I'd gotten myself into.

The truck was quiet aside from the sound of the rumbling engine. They didn't turn on any music and neither of them spoke, but there was a charge in the air. Their combined scents filled the cabin, and the brief reprieve I'd had from overpowering lust roared back full force. Unable to help myself, I placed a palm on each of their muscled thighs.

Each wore a tight t-shirt and denim, the hard muscle under my hands caused me to moan. Neither stopped me from touching them as I ran my hands up and down their hard forms. I unbuckled and turned my back to the windshield so that I could touch their chests, the muscle there just as firm. I absentmindedly licked my lips as my fingers roamed over them both.

I found myself anticipating arriving at their cabin and seeing what lay beneath their clothes. When my hands dipped lower, Zach grabbed my wrist, his voice nearly a groan.

"Wait, you need to be patient," he said.

Iavo looked over at his brother, a brow raised as if to say, *"Speak for yourself."*

I sat back down, embarrassed. Hurt. It felt like he'd rebuked me and I didn't like it. However, the longer I sat, the more I realized my hurt was more because I didn't want to stop touching them and not because he'd reprimanded me.

Nothing made sense. The moment I stopped touching them, I felt lost, empty. All I wanted was connection. Skin. I ached to feel them with every inch of my body.

Iavo must have sensed my longing, because he lifted me onto his lap and I curled up there like he'd just saved my life. The relief I felt was truly alarming. The trust. The complete and total willingness to give myself into his care.

The pull between myself and the twins was dangerous. I couldn't explain to myself why I was okay with the whole thing, but somehow, I was. I considered myself to be a clear-headed, confident, street-smart woman; going home with two strangers to have sex was not something a woman like that did. Too risky. Too dangerous.

We pulled onto a dirt path with a darkened cabin at the end. There were no lights on, inside or out. The surroundings were just as dark; the only thing I could see was a dirt road and the shaggy edges of pine trees when the headlights passed them.

When we parked, Iavo lifted me from the truck like I was

precious cargo. He kissed my temple before setting me gently on my feet. I followed the twins from the truck to their cabin, taking a deep breath as Zach unlocked the door and stepped inside.

The lights blazed on and I saw a comfortable space decorated like a Colorado ski resort, not a rundown cabin on the outer edges of Lake Michigan. I could smell the water, and a heavy fog hung over the forest surrounding the cabin like a gothic horror novel come to life.

Zach turned back to face me, waiting. Beside me in the dark, Iavo waited as well, silent and still like a predator, making me wonder if the vampire novels were true after all. There was something about these two that just didn't add up.

And, like vampires, they appeared to be waiting for me to *choose* to step over the threshold.

Was I going insane? Was this crazy?

I looked at Zach, at his muscles on top of muscles, his cut jaw and gorgeous green eyes. The lust I saw there was heady. No man had ever looked at me like that.

Looking over my shoulder at Iavo was a huge mistake. His eyes were amber, so vivid they almost looked like they were glowing in the reflection of the now bright porch light. He was staring but didn't touch me.

I wanted him to touch me. I wanted *both of them* to touch me. At the *same time.*

Maybe I was going to hell. Maybe I was about to be turned into some kind of mythical vampire junkie. I didn't care. I burned for them.

Zach had said that once I was inside their cabin, there would be no turning back.

He was wrong.

There had been no turning back the moment I saw them.

I took Iavo's hand and pulled him inside behind me. When the door slammed closed after him, I lifted my gaze to Zach and deliberately licked my lips.

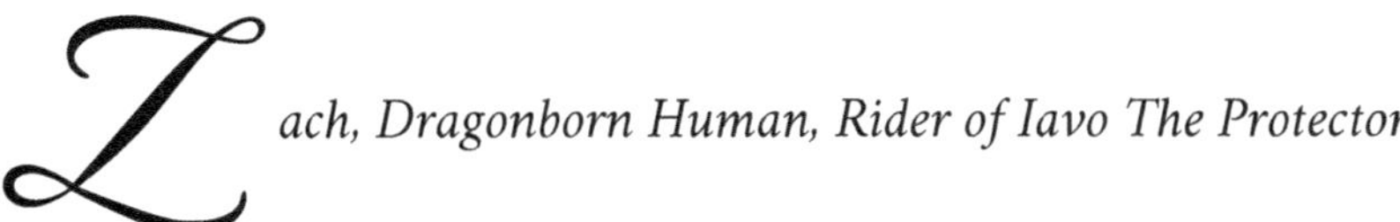

ach, Dragonborn Human, Rider of Iavo The Protector

BRITTANY WAS STUNNING, the type of beauty a man doesn't find often. Her beauty was honest and pure; she didn't fake anything or try to be something she wasn't. As my gaze fell on her now, her wide eyes peering at us with both trust and anticipation, I couldn't stop the overwhelming need to possess her from roaring through me. Possess. Claim. Mark as my own.

"You're ours now, Brittany." I wasn't referring to tonight, I meant forever, and I was furious at Iavo for not telling me at the bar. She was ours, our mate. She was Dragonborn, a descendant of a dragon, his rider and their human mate.

She was one of us. And she was ours.

Iavo stepped up behind her, his eyes blazing at me in defiance. I watched with envy as he slid his hands around her waist from behind and cupped her breasts in his palms. Her head fell back onto his shoulder in surrender and she closed her eyes, moaning as he rolled her nipples with his fingers.

"God, you smell so good. Why do you smell so good?" Her voice was husky with need and Iavo drew her scent deeply into his lungs, a growl coming from him as he dropped his lips to the side of her neck.

She is ready for us, Zach. Her wet heat calls me. The scent is like a drug. I won't be able to stop. Iavo's voice was gravelly, even inside my head.

"I don't think that's going to be an issue," I whispered, as I stepped closer and lowered my mouth to hers. Brittany gasped as I brushed the tips of my fingers along the sensitive skin of her curved hips and slid them around to cup her ass. She trembled as I pulled her towards me, parting her beautiful lips when I pressed mine against them.

Her golden hair was disheveled, but it was the type of messy that looked as though it had been done on purpose. It suited her and gave her a raw sexiness. My fingers twirled in her long locks as I kissed her harder.

Iavo lowered his hands to the hem of her shirt and I was forced to give up her mouth as he pulled the fabric off over her head. His fingers moved to toy with the straps of her white lace bra as he moved, kissing his way down her spine. She was trapped between us and based on the way she was clinging to my shoulders, she didn't want us to stop.

I kissed her like a drowning man and knew I would never get enough of her taste, the sounds she was making, the soft whimper of need as Iavo unhooked her bra and pulled the material down her arms.

Forced to lower her arms from my shoulders, she turned in surprise when Iavo held her hands locked at her sides, the bra straps acting as a binding. He took full advantage of her attention and stood up as she turned her head to look at him over her shoulder. He leaned forward and claimed her lips.

She let him hold her there, bound and on display, the feast before me one I knew Iavo had intended. Her breasts were bare, perfect, and thrust toward me, a perfect offering.

Like a magnet, her luxurious skin drew my gaze. She had a glow to her that I'd never really seen before. Her full, perky breasts begged to be touched and tasted, teased and pleasured. I wondered if the connection between her breasts and her clit was a strong one, or if she would be more aroused by other...activities.

Unable to wait another minute to taste her, I pulled her light pink nipple into my mouth and started to slowly suck it in and out of my mouth until the peak was even harder. She moaned as I sucked at the sensitive flesh, her mouth occupied by Iavo as he held her in place.

When she started to squirm, her hips thrusting forward... seeking...I kissed my way down to the waist of her jeans. Unbuttoned them. Slid them off her hips and made sure to take the small bit of silk panties with them.

She helped, wiggling her hips and kicking the pants off from where they had pooled around her ankles. All while Iavo held her. Kissed her. Made her shake and moan.

But I was not going to allow my selfish dragon to have all the fun. And a feast awaited.

Kneeling now, I lifted one leg over my shoulder and settled my tongue over her heated core.

With a gasp, she tore her mouth from Iavo to look down at me. I smiled just before sucking her sensitive clit into my mouth. Using one hand on her luscious ass to hold her in place, I ran the other up the inside of her thigh as I devoured her flesh, pressed two fingers deep.

Iavo watched her face with an intensity I, too, was feeling. Our mate was beautiful. Passionate. Naturally submissive. She made no effort to hide her pleasure, to stifle the whimpers of desire that filled the room.

With a smile, Iavo shifted slightly, still holding her hands in place, but moving to stand beside her, where he could lean down and feast on her perky breasts as I made her moan.

Iavo rubbed his hands down Brittany's firm body, stopping to caress her thighs and the intensely sensitive skin between the firm mounds of her bottom. After a few moments, he slowly slid a finger down to tease at her hot, tight hole. Before long, the beauty was grinding against my mouth, moaning as she wordlessly begged us for more.

I'm going to fuck her here, Zach. She's going to be so hot and tight around my cock, I can practically feel it already. She took my finger and wants more. I am going to give her more. Tell her. Tell her now. I ignored Iavo's mental command.

I was a bit too busy to be talking. The walls of her pussy were fluttering and pulsing around my fingers. She was moving in sync with my tongue, riding my mouth with a wild abandon that made me eager to throw her down on the floor and fuck her until she was mindless and screaming with release.

I worked her with my tongue and fingers, pumping them in and out of her as I suckled and rubbed the sensitive flesh in my mouth. It didn't take long.

"Yes!" Brittany bucked like a wild woman, her pussy clamping down on my fingers like a fist before going into a series of wild spasms that were so intense Iavo could feel them with the finger he had slipped inside her ass.

She's ours, Zach. Do you feel that? Her pussy knows she's ours. Her ass knows she's ours. I want her. Now. My dragon cock will bring her pussy more pleasure than your unskilled human tongue.

Finally willing to release her clit from my mouth, I kissed her thighs, then her stomach as she wilted in Iavo's hold. He held her effortlessly and I watched her with rapt attention as I answered the aggressive dragon forced to wait his turn. "She seems to like this human tongue just fine."

"God, you guys are so fucking hot." She was mumbling, limp and pliable in our eager hands.

Iavo released his hold on the bra straps and the feminine contraption fell to the ground at her feet. The moment his hand was free, he pulled her hair into a fist and angled her head back for a hard, deep kiss.

I want to fuck her. Now. Like this. Tell her.

Knowing I'd pushed him far enough, I complied, but not before taking her breasts into both hands and playing for a few seconds. "Iavo wants to lift you up and settle you on his hard cock. He wants to fuck you now, right here, while I hold you in place."

Her lips still locked to his kiss, she shuddered and blindly reached for my shoulder. When she made contact, she ripped her mouth from his to face me. "Yes. Fuck me. Do it."

He grunted in pleasure as he slid the tip of one finger inside of her then, his eyes closing when her tightness sheathed them completely. Over and over, he pumped in and out of her pussy, harder and faster.

She moaned and grabbed my hair to pull my lips closer—which I loved. When she grabbed my free hand and lowered it to her clit, I smiled and played. I adored her assertiveness. There was nothing sexier in the world than a woman who knew what she wanted and wasn't afraid to ask for it.

I slid my fingers across her wet clit as Iavo fucked her from behind. He pushed deep, driving her onto my fingers as he stretched her open. Filled her.

Dragon magic filled the air, the heat of fire and scent of dragon rising around us for the first time in our lives together. I'd only tasted this kind of magic from Iavo once before, when his egg had hatched and he'd bonded to me.

But that was different. An understanding between warriors. This was something else. This was sex and heat and lust, and it drove us wild, filled our heads with mindless need.

All inhibition was lost and I stepped back, bending her over as Iavo pumped into her body. I lowered Brittany's head to my hard cock, praying she'd let me fuck her hot, wet mouth.

She obliged, wrapping her hands around the base and sucking me deep. A sharp gasp stuck in her throat as my hard length hit the back of her throat. She smiled as she started to stroke up and down, moaning as she shifted position so she could get her mouth closer to me as Iavo continued to fill her from behind.

I threw my head back and let the pleasure build. Yet, it was my turn to give the orders. "Wrap around her and get your fingers on her clit, Iavo. Make her come. Make her scream with my cock in her mouth."

Those perfect lips of hers parted and her tongue licked the head, swirling it around the tip several times. "Yes, Iavo. Do it." She then opened her mouth wide and swallowed me down. I about choked on my own gasp when I realized just how deep she could take me, and I couldn't wait to test her limits. It was a good fucking thing that I wasn't a dragon, because I would have accidentally set the room on fire.

"Your mouth is so hot, mate. Take all of me. Suck me harder." Who was begging now?

Iavo laughed through our telepathic link, but his humor faded the moment his body wrapped around hers, his hand dove under her belly, and his fingers found Brittany's clit. I don't know exactly what he did to her, but she bucked and moaned, the vibration of her throat on the head of my cock nearly making me stumble.

I enjoyed watching her body quiver and jolt, as the pleasure traveled up her long, silky body. The taste of her remained on my tongue, her sweet scent filling the room as Iavo worked her body like a master.

I moaned out, calling her name as I could feel myself about to explode, and pulled out just in time to not lose my load inside her mouth. I wanted to fill her with my seed, mark her as my own, as Iavo was doing.

I pushed her upright once more. She was still riding Iavo's cock and I held her steady until she wrapped her feet and ankles behind Iavo's knees. She was almost sitting on him now and I shoved his hand out of the way so I could rub my hard cock up and over her swollen clit to her stomach. Over and over, I rubbed my swollen head up and down her wetness, teasing us both before I leaned in to kiss her.

Iavo pumped into her, harder and faster. I knew the moment he exploded, lost control, made her ours, because she tore her lips from mine and screamed. The orgasm was so strong I could feel her entire lower abdomen pulsing against the length of my cock where it was pressed between us. Dragon magic was strong. Not only would it bring our mate the ultimate pleasure, but each time she accepted us into her body, took our magic and our seed, she would be more attracted to us. She would need us. Want us. But not until the final claiming, when she took us both at the same time, me deeply into her pussy and Iavo in her ass, when I filled her with human seed and Iavo filled her with dragon magic, would she truly be ours by the laws and customs of the Dragonborn. But she would take us both, and then she would be ours.

Forever.

We would have sons and daughters. Future dragon riders and future mates of the Dragonborn came from unions such as this.

Lust. Need. Magic.

I watched pleasure fill her face and felt something elemental shift within me. She was beautiful in her release, wild and uninhibited. Passionate. *Mine.* I'd never wanted a woman before, not like this. I would hunt for her. Kill for her. Die for her.

"Mine." The word was little more than a growl as I lifted her still quivering body even higher, forcing Iavo's cock to slip free from her wet pussy. Tired of standing up, I carried her to the bed and laid her down on her back. I had my clothes off in seconds, but Iavo was faster. He was next to her, working her pussy with one hand while he feasted on her breasts with his mouth. The picture of my dragon and my mate locked in such intimate pleasure on the bed stunned me briefly, but I moved forward and knelt between her legs, once more shoving the eager dragon's hand out of my way. This pussy was mine now. Mine.

"Brittany?" I still needed permission. She'd taken Iavo, but he'd asked. She had to take us both. She had to *choose* to accept both of us.

Fingers buried in Iavo's hair as he sucked at her nipple, she arched her back off the bed and spread her knees wider. "Yes. Fuck me. Do it. I want you."

Lifting myself, I pressed my throbbing cock against her opening before thrusting deep. She was wet with her own arousal as well as Iavo's dragon elixir. His cock had evolved for fucking a willing female in the ass, for filling his mate with magic anywhere, anytime. He did not fill his mate with seed. Instead, his elixir acted as a magical bonding agent, ensuring any offspring would be compatible with dragon blood, both mates and riders for future generations of his kind. He was self-lubricating, which made Brittany's pussy a hot, wet haven.

Iavo held her in place as I pushed forward, thrusting deep. I took her hips in my hands to lift her a bit higher as I pumped myself in and out of her wetness. She whimpered, moaned and pulled Iavo in for a kiss. I slid in and out of her glorious folds. I could feel her wetness dripping down my balls as I pressed against her deeper, and deeper.

Until it wasn't enough. I settled her back down on the bed and pushed her knees up and out, spreading her open as far as she could go. She moaned and bucked against the sheer width of my cock in the new position and I slid in deeper.

Iavo held her down, his hands on her breasts and he kissed

her. Neither of us willing to let her regain her senses, her control.

Hold her open and fuck her hard. I'll make her come. I want her to come. Now. I want to watch her face when she loses control. Iavo was being his aggressive, arrogant dragon-self again, but we were in perfect agreement. I wanted to watch her scream. No, I wanted to *make* her scream. I wanted to feel the walls of her pussy milking my cock. I wanted my seed deep inside her. Iavo had marked her with his elixir. It was my turn to fill her up. Make my claim.

I did as he said, fucking her hard and faster. Deeper. Each thrust rocking her body on the bed, making her perfect breasts bounce as Iavo reached down and stroked her clit faster than my human eyes could track.

Her back came up off the bed as she rocked and screamed, her pussy pulsing like a clenched fist around my hard length.

I lost control; my own release rocketed through me from toes to balls, my cum pouring out of me as I fought not to collapse on top of her.

When the spasms were done, I slowly, reluctantly, pulled out of her wet heat and laid down on the bed beside her. Iavo was on her other side and we quickly pressed her between us where she would be warm and protected. Safe.

Ours.

I shall take first watch over our mate. Sleep, Zach.

Within moments, Brittany was sleeping. Iavo needed very little sleep. He had guarded my slumber for years. I knew that now, with a mate to protect, he would be twice as vigilant.

No one fucked with a dragon protecting his mate. At least

not any sane creature, human or otherwise. Anyone threatening Brittany now had a serious death wish.

And that included the Riven we'd been sent here to hunt. With our mate here, Iavo's instinct to hunt and destroy the other dragon would be nearly impossible to control. Not that I would hold him back. I wanted the Riven dead so we could focus on softer—I ran my hand up and down Brittany's soft hip and thigh—more pleasurable things.

Stop being a girl and go to sleep. We hunt at dawn.

Bossy bastard, but I agreed. The sooner we eliminated the rogue dragon, the sooner we could take our mate, go home to the desert and get out of this miserable fucking cold.

 rittany

AS DIFFICULT AS it was to leave the comfort and safety the two, gorgeous men offered, I needed to find my brother. I got dressed and reached into my pocket, making sure the piece of paper was still there. I kissed them both good-bye. Iavo, the silent one, wrapped his hand around my wrist, but his twin snarled something and Iavo let me go. I felt a little sad as I closed the door, but no matter how amazing the night before had been, or how much I longed to crawl back in bed and forget everything with the twins, it was just a one-night stand. Stupid to think it was anything else. Just stupid. And I'd given up on lying to myself a long time ago.

I made my way to the street and used my app to get a taxi. The driver took me back to my car so I could drive across the city to my brother's dorm. A lot of driving, but I welcomed the delay. My heart was in my throat as the nervousness from the day before returned. I was truly worried he'd tell me to get lost, and I wasn't exactly sure how I would handle that.

The ride through the city was turbulent—frequent stops and starts, racecar worth lane changes and a driver who sped like a madman, darting between cars and semi-trucks alike. For some reason, the young taxi driver thought I was in an extreme hurry to get there, but I wasn't at all. As much as I wanted to get this over with, for better or worse, and just be able to see my baby brother again, I needed some time to calm myself before I got there. The driver, however, had other plans, and I buckled in after the third time I was thrown sideways across the backseat.

When we pulled up outside the restaurant, my stomach was roiling from motion-sickness. Or anxiety. Maybe a bit of both. Then, Mr. Hot Wheels cleared his throat and broke me from my moment of peace.

Once I was on campus and pulled up in front of the dorm, I sat there staring at the building, doing my best to calm my head. After a few minutes, I got out and stared at the nine-story brick building in front of me, my hands repeatedly balling into fists before stretching and repeating the process, trying to relieve the tension I felt in my body. I reached for the piece of paper with his address on it. I had assumed the number was his room number and the name *Scott* in the street location was the dorm.

I was standing in front of a three-story building with a sign reading *Scott Lawson Hall*, so I assumed I was in the right place.

Walking inside, I got into the elevator, pushed the button for the third floor, and started shadow boxing, shuffling my feet. I was doing my best to get myself revved up. If there had been another person on the elevator, I couldn't have done it, but I needed a big dose of courage right now—and the ride to my car in the death-defying taxi hadn't helped calm my nerves.

When the doors opened, I took the first step out, trying to ground myself. When I felt steady, I made my way down the hall. Standing in front of his door, I brought my hand up and down several times before taking a deep breath and knocking.

The sound of footsteps approaching from inside made my heart thud heavily in my chest. Soon, I heard the handle move, and the door opened. The guy who answered the door looked at me through squinty, bloodshot eyes. The smell of marijuana came flowing towards me, and I briefly wondered if he were my brother, but just looking at him I knew he wasn't. This guy was a lot shorter than me with dreadlocks and a goatee.

"Is Garrett here?" I asked. My voice threatened to crack, but I wouldn't let it.

"No, he's gone, you know, shopping." The guy grinned as he spoke and started to close the door in my face, but I wasn't about to let that go.

Taking a step forward, I said, "Shopping? Great, can you tell me where?"

I was thinking I could go see if I could pick him out in a store with strangers. I put my foot in the door as he continued to close it.

"Look he's just out, okay? I'm not supposed to talk to his ladies anyway. I've already said too much, but I was high. You caught me off guard, way to go."

I sighed. "So, he's out with a girl I'm guessing?"

"I don't know." The roommate crossed his arms and turned

his nose up in the air as he shook his head no. "I'm not his babysitter, you know?"

I was about to lose my shit. I didn't go through all the mental anguish over this for so long just so I could have some jackass slam a door in my face.

I slapped my hand against the door then, giving a rude, forced smile that I hoped he'd catch the true meaning of. "Just tell me where he is. I'm not a floozy, although it seems he must have a few of them. I'm his sister." I was beyond frustrated with the kid and not in the mood to beat around the bush anymore.

"Oh," the guy looked taken aback. "He never mentioned having a sister. He's hooking up with a girl. They went home together last night. He should be back in a couple hours. Probably sleeping it off, you know?"

"Okay. Now we're getting somewhere." I debated on whether I should leave a message. I felt like it would be better to just see him in person, and I was starving. Now that I knew I wouldn't be able to talk to him anytime soon, my stomach decided to be angry with me for skipping breakfast.

"You do know what I mean by hooking up, right?" the guy unnecessarily continued.

My eyes narrowed as I looked him over. Was he serious? "Yes, you ass, I do."

"Sorry. Just asking. You look kinda old-fashioned." The guy gave a shrug and lifted his bong to his lips—not even bothering to leave the doorway—and I found myself wondering if my brother smoked as much weed as his roommate, or was as rude? *Old-fashioned?* I'd just *hooked up* with two of the hottest men I'd ever seen, complete strangers I'd picked up in a bar.

So, who was I to judge? Ugh. Rolling my eyes, I asked, "Where's the best place to get breakfast around here?"

"It's Addie's Bakery for sure. If you want, I'll take you there." The guy pushed his bangs out of the way so I could see him wiggle his brows. "They have awesome donuts with lots of frosting." His gaze travelled over my ample curves, which, I had to admit, revealed my sweet tooth with a bit too much junk in the trunk. In the bra. Hell, a bit too much to hold onto everywhere.

"Thanks, but I can find it myself."

His frown was comical, as if he'd never been turned down before. "Whatever. I've got the munchies, and you're kinda hot. So, we could get donuts and then work off the sugar high together – if you know what I mean."

He was going to get a punch if he didn't watch it. Especially after what I'd experienced the night before. I was relatively certain no man could live up to Zach and Iavo ever again. Still, I managed to hold back my irritation. The kid was stoned, horny, and way too young for me. I needed a man in my bed—or two. Thinking about Iavo and Zach now made my nipples hard and my pussy pulse with heat. I wanted them again. Already. Which, after the number of orgasms I'd had last night, should be impossible. "No thank you. I've got GPS. I'll be back later."

He nodded. "Should I tell Garrett his sister stopped by?"

"No, I want to surprise him. I'll come back by after lunch. Surely, he'll be back by then." With that, I bid my brother's high roomie goodbye and headed off to find breakfast.

Zach

Iavo continued to glare at me as he had been since Brittany walked out the door. He was concerned with her being out in the world with a Riven nearby. It was also possible he simply wanted to be near her. Which wasn't an option at the moment.

"Knock off the hate, Iavo. You know we need to go find the Riven before he does any more damage. Think with your head and not your dick for a few hours."

She should be back at the cabin with the doors and windows locked.

I burst into laughter. "She's not a prisoner. She's our mate. And there's no food at the cabin."

She does not understand that she is mine, that I will provide for her.

"Ours, dragon. She's our mate. And she'll be fine. She's miles away from here looking for her brother. She'll be safer there than at the cabin with your scent all over her. That's just the sort of temptation a Riven doesn't need." I hated to remind Iavo of the obvious, but he was truly out of sorts, not thinking clearly. I'd heard that dragons were difficult to manage when they found their mate, but Iavo was normally so analytical and cold that I teased him that ice flowed in his dragon veins instead of fire. But not any longer, not when it came to *her.*

Not that I could argue or was doing much better. Her scent clung to my skin and I could still hear her soft cries of pleasure as we'd seduced her soft body, made her come over and over again pressed between us. Thinking about the softness of her skin, the wet heat of her core, made my cock grow hard with longing. I wanted more. Needed more. Just like my dragon. But I wasn't an animal, I was a man; a man determined to control my base urges and focus on the task at hand.

"Today we hunt. *Tonight,* we seduce our mate."

We'll take to the air and look for him, Iavo thought to me. Even his internal voice had an edge, as if he truly were fighting for control.

"She'll be fine," I reassured him again as we set out to find a good place for him to shift into his dragon form.

Once we were within the cover of the trees, he allowed the power to swell around him as his aura shifted, letting his human body change into that of the great dragon. Iavo hated being in human form, and if he was given any chance to assume his true form, he did. His amber and gold scales glistened in the early morning sun as he stretched his legs out. I hopped on the wing he'd lowered down enough for me to easily climb up and grabbed a couple of hard scales as he took off into the air.

"What are you looking for exactly?" I asked hoping he had a plan.

I'll know when I feel it. I'll know where he is.

I looked down along the edge of the lake, searching for any sign of a dragon or anything that seemed out of place. My eyes saw nothing, but that didn't mean anything. Iavo was the one with the extra senses.

I sense a dragon. I can't tell if he's the Riven, but he's close.

"There's a cave. Do you think that's where he is?" I pointed.

As an answer, Iavo cut sharp and slanted sideways as he descended. Having changed direction without warning, I nearly lost my balance and had to lean forward, wrapping my arms around his neck. His scales pressed painfully into me, but I held tight anyway.

I knew he'd done it on purpose, for whatever reason, but there was no time to be angry about it. We were fast approaching the cave, and it didn't look like it would have a large enough space to accommodate his size.

"Iavo!" I yelled at him when he didn't slow down and flew straight for the cave. "You won't fit!"

He was flying wildly, his wings tilting back and forth as he weaved. It was making me a bit nauseous, though I'd never admit it to him. He made himself go faster, and right before he hit the cave, he shot straight up in the air, cutting a huge flip and letting me off on the ground right at the edge of the lake.

He thought he was so damn funny.

Landing just outside the cave, he knocked me off my feet with a blast of air from his wings. My heart was racing, and I did my best to shake off the jittery feeling after his not so subtle message. He was angry that we'd left Brittany alone.

Climbing to my feet, I brushed off the wet grass from my ass and thighs and glared at him but didn't say anything. There was no point. Iavo loved trying to get under my skin. Dragons weren't pets, they were mythical creatures that breathed ice and fire, with tempers to match. And Iavo wasn't just a dragon, he was a dragon who needed his mate.

"We serve the queen first, Iavo."

His massive head swung toward me, the amber jewels of his eyes narrowed. *She is my queen. My mother. Do not think to give me orders,* human.

Whoa. He was testier than I thought. He hadn't called me *human* in years. I placed my hand just beneath his eye and stared right back at him. "I miss her, too. But unless we kill this Riven, Brittany will never be safe."

He snorted and the ground in front of his nose blackened as a patch of vegetation turned to ash. *That is the only reason I am here. But she would be safer in my bed.*

"Our bed." Why was I constantly reminding Iavo that she was my mate as well? The dragon chose the mate. Period. But despite the fact that Iavo had seen her first, I found that I was just as possessive, just as determined to protect her. And just as irritable when she wasn't near. I was a mess, just like my dragon, falling in love with a complete stranger in just one night. Now that I knew Brittany was in the world, I simply could not imagine living without her.

I didn't have the senses my dragon possessed, so I couldn't tell when a Dragonborn was near. I relied on the prickly feel at the nape of my neck or the feeling of being watched. At the moment, I only felt irritation that my ass had gotten wet when Iavo threw me to the ground.

Moving down the bank, I had to wade into the water to reach the mouth of the cave. A burst of cold air hit me the closer I got, letting me know I was in the right place. I looked over my shoulder at Iavo, who shook his large dragon head. *The Riven is not here. He is close, but the cave is empty.*

Trusting his senses, I made my way to the entrance of the cave and stepped inside. The first thing I saw was a dress lying on the ground. The fabric was black and gold, and it looked to have been made by an expensive designer. A diamond tennis bracelet lay nearby and some other jeweled trinkets, such as cufflinks, earrings, and even someone's ear with a sapphire stud of at least two carats still attached, had been pushed into a small pile, as if the dragon was a jewelry collector.

I shuddered and moved back, wondering exactly what we might be dealing with here. No matter how much death I'd seen in Riven lairs over the years, I never got used to it. A little past the pile of treasure, I saw the body of an elderly man, naked and frozen stiff. It had been pushed up against the wall of the cave, still standing. I couldn't make out any features because it was facing away from me.

I turned to move away from the morbid scene and tripped over another body. This one appeared to be a man in his forties. Another half dozen bodies lined the walls of the Riven's den as if he used them for decoration, or furniture. The second body had a row of icicles hanging off one of his ears in a perfectly straight line. His mouth lay open and his tongue had frosted over.

I scrunched up my face, expecting to smell decay, but there wasn't any death odor in the cave. They were perfectly preserved underneath their ice coffins. A woman of similar age lay next to him. She wasn't wearing a top, and her breasts had frozen right to the ice. I found myself wondering if the Riven froze them while they were alive. The way the man's mouth hung open in a silent scream, it was a strong possibility.

Looking around the cave, I tried to see if the dragon had left any trace of himself or clues to where he might have gone. The rest of the frozen corpses were well dressed, and from the jewelry they wore, I determined they had money. From the items lying around *without* a human body still attached, I decided *all* the victims had money. So, the Riven could have been taking victims from a casino, a fancy night club, or maybe a rich neighborhood in the city.

Either way, he was certainly in a killing mood. It didn't seem he'd eaten that many people, but it was hard to tell. On top of the anxiety about the Riven we were dealing with, I began to feel the itching sensation begging me to get back to Brittany. I couldn't shake the urgency that we needed to go. *Right now.*

Leaving everything untouched, I walked back out to Iavo, who stood guard at the cave's entrance. "There are seven bodies in there. They're definitely the work of our boy; frozen solid."

There are bodies out here, too. Come. I'll show you.

I stared at him incredulously for a moment. "You just want to toss me off again."

Smiling, he thought, *Always, but I will behave. Come.*

With a sigh and a shake of my head, I jumped on Iavo's back. As he took off, he lurched to the left and flew down to the water to an area with a thick patch of trees.

Iavo flew up over them and looked down. I did the same and saw a sheet of ice the size of a hockey rink there inside the tree line. Somehow, the trees were growing straight up through the ice, but I didn't think they'd survive buried in frost for very long.

Beneath the ice, there were more bodies, a lot of them. I was a little shocked at how busy the Riven had been. As terrifying as it was, this was truly impressive. I'd seen this level of carnage before, but never from just one dragon. This Riven was truly off his dragon rocker.

"He's been killing since he got here," I said just after we landed again. I hopped down and looked around, staying close to my dragon. "He's posted up I guess. We need to figure out where he is sleeping."

In my past experiences with the Riven, they very rarely slept where they ate. The bodies piling up didn't make a comfortable place to stay. There was one case where a Riven took over a mansion and used specific rooms to store his kills, but that wasn't the case most of the time.

The Riven watches us. I can feel his presence.

"I know, Iavo, but I don't see him."

He is hiding from me, as he should.

Nothing like a little dragon arrogance. In this case, it was well-deserved. Iavo was the queen's favorite and most feared hunter. Me, she tolerated. But Iavo was her son. "If he's hiding, he's not killing. Do your thing. Let's track him down. Brittany has been on her own for too long."

Now he sees reason. Iavo climbed higher, heading for a bank of clouds we could use for cover as we searched the rest of the lake. *Or perhaps you, too, are thinking with your cock.*

"Shut-up or I'll keep her to myself."

It is my fire she needs.

"Yeah, well, she's human and I've got the sperm your queen needs to make new little dragon riders, so behave." A dragon could not impregnate his human mate, but shared dragon fire, spreading magic through his mate's body, magic that bound the unborn child to the dragons, that made the baby Dragonborn, future mate or rider.

I did have the sensation of being watched as I clung to Iavo's back. The hair on the back of my neck stood up, and I had cold chills. If I didn't know better, I'd say the Riven was right behind us. Turning, I saw nothing but the lake and the sky stretched out for miles.

I didn't see the dragon attack. It rose from beneath us like a great white in the sea and scored Iavo's chest with his massive claws.

Iavo screamed in rage, rolling to his side to avoid the rest of the attack as the pale blue ice dragon's rear talons missed his head, his neck, by inches.

Roaring in challenge, Iavo straightened and started his pursuit. Away from land, out over the cold water where I would become a liability, and the ice dragon would have a massive tactical advantage.

"No, Iavo. Go back."

I shall strip the meat from his bones with my teeth, breathe his body to ash and pound those ashes into the ground. Iavo was beyond logic, in a killing rage. In pain. Openly challenged by another of his kind. By a dragon with no rider, nothing to temper the violence running through his veins. Nothing to temper the grief of losing his rider.

Had the ice dragon been mated, his woman may have been able to stabilize him, help him survive long enough to choose another rider. But alone, the dragon had become Riven. Remorseless. Evil. Living only to kill. No matter how much blood he spilled, it would never be enough to fill the emptiness inside him.

Going Riven was the only thing a dragon truly feared.

Iavo's dragon blood flowed up over his shoulder from the wound, a small amount of the liquid defying gravity as the wind pushed it up and over his bulk due to the speed of Iavo's flight. I'd seen him like this only once before. And on that hunt, we'd pursued the dragon to its den, fought covered in blood. There had been no reason to turn back, to deny the risk.

We'd had nothing to lose.

"Iavo, go back. We must return to Brittany. We have a mate. The bonding has begun. We are following that asshole into a trap and we both know it. We have to think of Brittany."

I sensed the change in my dragon's body, the battle rage leaving his form slowly, inch by inch, until his fuming dragon heart stopped pounding and only the sound of his wings in the wind remained.

For Brittany. I will heal. Then we will hunt again.

"He dies. He's a threat to our mate."

Iavo roared into the air one last time and turned, climbing above the clouds, so high we would not be taken by surprise a second time as he sped back to our cabin. *Yes, the traitor must die.*

CHAPTER 4

rittany, Lincoln Park, Chicago

THE LIGHT EVENING breeze blew through the tall trees, the dead leaves shaking at me as I walked on the narrow stretch of sidewalk that ran along the grass. Off to my left, huge gray rocks covered in graffiti separated a stretch of dead, brown grass from the water of Lake Michigan. Normally, walking along the water's edge made me feel peaceful and gave me a chance to think. It wasn't that late and soon I'd be back to the busier area, where I could hear people shouting for their kids to come along. This was my escape; the place I came to get away from the everyday bullshit that was my life. This was where I drove without thinking when I'd returned to Garrett's dorm and he still wasn't home.

Usually, this place gave me a sense of peace. Hope. Tonight, I felt like eyes were on me. And not of the friendly variety.

My ears tuned into the ambient sounds around me, attempting to pick something out of the nothing. There were no footsteps. No voices. There seemed to be no one here, but I couldn't shake the sensation that I was being hunted. Which was stupid, but I'd never been one to ignore my instincts.

The tree in front of me creaked, groaning as it swayed as if to say, *Hurry, Brittany, it's not safe for you here.* A shiver clawed its way down my body. I didn't have a clue where the nervous energy came from, but I wished it would pass—and quickly.

Picking up the pace, I interlocked my hands in front of me, twirling my index fingers while humming a made-up tune to keep myself company. The tree groaned again, and I stared, making my way over to its massive trunk. I stopped and looked up, my eyes looking from thick branch to thick branch. From underneath, it seemed to have no end, as if it stretched into the sky and beyond the clouds.

My instincts piqued again, and another chill ran through me. The back of my neck prickled, and I quickly turned to see if someone was behind me. The thought of someone watching me, hiding in bushes and following me as I walked, turned from concern to full blown paranoia.

Something wasn't right—but should I run? Or act like nothing was happening. Would I provoke an attack if I ran? Or if I didn't? Maybe whatever was out there was just evil, and not paying any attention to me.

My stomach roiled as my mouth filled with saliva. Bending over with my hands on my knees, I took deep breaths until the nausea passed. It was time to get out of the park. Running would have been obvious—though spinning around with wide eyes and searching the area wasn't much better.

I didn't care. I took off at a sprint, not slowing until I reached the parking lot, and people, and my waiting car. Walking quickly to my car, I didn't look behind me. I could still feel the eyes on me and didn't want to give whoever or whatever it was the idea they needed to follow me.

Part of me screamed that I was being ridiculous and paranoid, but I knew I wasn't. Someone was out there, watching me. I hoped when I left they'd lose interest and go somewhere else.

I climbed into my old Buick and locked all the doors. Resting my head on the steering wheel, I leaned back and something poked me in the side. Startled, I screamed, my eyes darting over to see a straw from a fast food cup had been the culprit. The drink inside had spilled into the center console —*fantastic*. My car was a complete disaster area, and I made a promise to myself to clean it before I went back to try to see my baby brother.

I fumbled with the keys to properly place them in the ignition and start the engine. Several times I missed, catching the entire set of keys in my hand only to have to separate the car key from the others before trying again.

I closed my eyes, making a silent wish for my poor old car. The back end had been rammed by not one, but two cars in parking lots. The offending drivers hadn't even bothered to stick around once it happened, so it was a miracle the bumper was still holding on. A green door now disturbed the nice black color. I'd had to have it put on after another wreck took the back-driver's side door out. It wasn't nice to look at, but it got me where I needed to go.

As I finally got my nervous hands to cooperate, I shoved the key in the ignition, hoping it would start and take me away from this place and away from the current source of my anxiety. There was always a chance it wouldn't start, and I held my breath every time I turned the key.

My stomach growled, and though the nausea hadn't dissipated completely, I was well aware of every single thing I'd eaten for breakfast churning inside me. The grease-soaked bacon had tasted fantastic, but I regretted it now.

The car started and relief washed over me, a cautious smile breaking out on my worry-torn face.

Putting it into drive, I pulled out onto the road, the anxiety and the feeling like I was being followed still plagued me. My gaze continued to hop from one mirror to the next. There hadn't been anyone else walking along that path, and there wasn't a single car around me now.

Going somewhere familiar, somewhere I felt safe, I pulled a piece of paper with my brother's last known address on it from the dash and smoothed it over the steering wheel. It was worn from folding and unfolding every time I took it out of my pocket. The ink was starting to fade and the paper was becoming thin and fragile.

Garrett had only been eight when a family took him in and raised him to be normal, or at least what I had assumed would be normal, given the Midwestern address. It was the last time I had seen him, and he was the lucky one.

After all the time that had passed, it was hard to imagine him as a college student. He was frozen in time in my mind as an adorable, funny, little eight-year-old boy. Seeing him again would be like meeting a whole new person. It *would* be meeting a whole new person. His life, his experiences... They would have changed him, shaped him into someone I didn't know at all. Someone I'd never met.

The more I thought about it, the more intimidated by the situation I became. I had a deep fear he wouldn't want to have anything to do with me. It had been many years and it was completely possible he'd scrubbed me, and our loser parents, completely from his mind. Being that young, it would be the best coping mechanism he could have hoped for. Letting us go would have allowed him to move on with his life—but I hoped he still held a place in his heart for me.

When the rear-view mirror stayed empty, I let myself breathe again.

Good.

Time to go back over to my brother's dorm and try again. I'd come halfway across the country to find him. I wasn't going to give up because his roommate liked to ramble when he was stoned.

Iavo, The Protector, First of His Name

SHOULDER CLIPPED and bleeding from our encounter with the ice dragon, I landed in the field behind our rented cabin and waited impatiently for Zach to get the hell off my back.

The moment his feet hit the ground, I called the Earth's magic to me and shifted forms, into a man identical in looks to my rider. But I was naked and bleeding, and in no mood to talk, not when the traitor who'd attacked us still lived.

"You've looked better." Zach slapped me on the back, careful to avoid the large gash across my chest and shoulder.

It'll heal. I need a shower. I answered as I always did, mind-to-mind. I could not speak as the humans did. When I was younger, that fact had annoyed me. Now I realized the gift it was, not being forced to endure conversation with the humans I protected.

I shrugged off Zach's hand and walked to the cabin. We didn't bother to lock the door, as we would both know instantly if our lodgings had been disturbed. Dragon senses came in handy once in a while.

I turned the water on as hot as it would flow and stepped into the antique tub, pulling the clean but worn white shower curtain closed.

"Hurry up in there," Zach shouted through the closed door. "We can't let him get too far."

I must heal.

"Well, do it fast."

Rolling my eyes, I allowed the hot water to run over me, washing away the stench of blood and burn and dragon fire as my body healed. There was nowhere on this planet I could not track a fellow dragon. It could take time, if the dragon was smart, but I was one of the greatest hunters alive. Precisely the reason our queen had chosen me for this mission.

I probably should have hurried, but I hurry for no one. My human rider, Zachary Matthias Murray, could wait. It was almost dark and he wanted to fly north, over the cold expanse of Lake Michigan, and continue our hunt for the Riven. We'd get there soon enough.

After taking my time, relishing the heat, but despising the fact that the water never felt hot enough, I rinsed myself, pulled the towel from the rack, and dried off. Once I was dry, I hung the towel back up, and ran my hands through my blond hair to tame it, even if only slightly.

Even though Zach and I look like twins, his hair listened a hell of a lot better than mine did. When I exited the bathroom, Zach was sitting in the teal plush chair in the living room next to the bathroom door. His gaze immediately sought the wound on my shoulder. Which was gone.

"Good. You're healed."

Of course.

"Then let's go get this bastard."

He wanted us to hunt the Riven. I had other needs. I needed to hunt our mate, to find her, fill her, claim her over and over until her body was coated in my scent, my heat.

If Zach thought to keep me from my mate, or deny that she was ours, this Riven we hunted would not be the only one who needed killing.

I was close to the edge, hanging on by force of will alone. I hid the worst of it from Zach, despite the fact that our telepathic bond made it impossible for me to keep everything from him. My moods colored his, and when, in the past, I had ached for our mate, he'd become dark and brooding, throwing women at me, hoping a one-night-stand would appease the monster growing within.

Nothing helped. There was only one female on this Earth

destined to be ours. And I needed to be with her before the fire in my blood grew beyond my control.

To keep from having another meaningless conversation, I focused my eyes anywhere but on him. It was easy to do while getting dressed. I quickly pulled on a pair of jeans, grabbed a black t-shirt, and stepped into my boots before we made our way to the door. We would track the Riven on land, at least for a while.

The weather was colder than I liked, which wasn't saying much as I preferred the heat on any given day. But the damp air soaked into my fire dragon's bones like claws, making me ache all over, especially when I was in this small, weak, human form. But humans didn't respond well to dragons flying around, spewing fire and ripping each other to shreds. There weren't many of my kind left. Fewer each year. More lost to the darkness inherent in our kind. The dragons who had survived the last war were old and frail, failing. And the new generation, the others like me, were having trouble finding the Dragonborn females who could successfully breed the next generation of riders. Our mates, who could give birth to men like Zach. Men born with dragon blood.

I followed my rider out into the chill night air, the cold making me even more irritable than taking a dragon talon across the shoulder had. *"Must we do this now? It's fucking cold,"* I complained in my head to Zach. I didn't mind the hunt, but what I wanted was a warm meal and an even warmer woman in our bed. Our mate was near. I could feel it in my blood, my magic all but shouting at me to go back to her, take her to bed and officially claim her before another dragon found her first.

Dragonborn females were rare. Valuable. And always beautiful. Though they rarely knew what they were, what their birthright would mean, until their dragon and rider claimed them.

I couldn't wait to teach Brittany what it would truly mean to be mine.

"Ours, Iavo. You will have to share her."

Only if you beg, human.

Zach laughed, but rolled his eyes at me before saying, "I want her, too, but we must hunt tonight. The Riven was injured as well. He will be hungry. We have to find him before he kills again. Your cock will have to wait."

Easy for you to say. Zach didn't feel what I did, the burning in my blood, the constant edge of fury running through every cell, the need to hunt. To find *her.* To taste her sweet pussy and fill her with my hard…

"If we don't kill this bastard, our mate will never be safe. You know that." I could hear Zach's warning as he turned and started walking toward the trail that led from our lodgings to the lake.

He was correct. Only I could choose our mate, a mate with dragon blood, but now that I had, Zach and I would share her. She would be bound to both of us, by magic and blood, part of us. And unless we killed this Riven, no one would be safe, including Brittany.

But I didn't care about the rest of the world. I only cared about her. *Fine. Let's hunt him and see it done.* The sooner I killed the evil dragon the faster I could return to the only thing that mattered, the hunt for *her.*

"It's cold." Zach grumbled as I followed him down the

narrow path. It was dark now, the winter wind snapping at our flesh like metal whips.

It was my turn then to shake my head and roll my eyes. He was wearing a coat, gloves, and heavy winter gear. I wore little, needing to be able to shift to dragon form quickly. *Thanks for the weather report,* I responded in my head as I stepped in front of him and cranked up my internal heat. He fell into step behind me, absorbing the magical warmth I provided. Or using me for a wind block. Probably both. But that was our way, our duty to one another. Dragon to Rider. Rider to Dragon. Where one went, so did the other. When one suffered, both suffered. From the day of our bonding, we lived or died together.

If something happened to Zach, I would follow him into the eternal night. I was strong enough to make the choice. I refused to become what we hunted. A Riven. A dragon whose soul was lost to evil. Dragons lived and died with our honor intact.

Or we were hunted down and removed from the world. As we should be.

The Riven was weak, and deserved the end I would give him.

"Thanks." Zach's teeth weren't rattling when he spoke, so I took it as a sign of improvement. And since no response was needed, I held my tongue.

"Keep your eyes open; the Riven could be anywhere."

Without speaking, I looked around the path. I was glad for any distraction from the cold. We kept walking, winding around the lake. The path went up and around a small hill then straight down into the water.

Let's wait until late, after the humans have taken to their beds.

Then we can take to the skies, I thought. Zach nodded in response and kept walking as we came to the edge of the water.

"I hope he's not waiting for us out there," Zach said, a shiver that he didn't attempt to hide racing over his body.

I kicked a boulder, it rolled down the cliff and into the gentle waves below. Small slices of ice clung to the shoreline, the water most likely frigid. I shuddered. Even in the springtime, Lake Michigan was far too cold. As I stood there, dreading the thought of battling an ice dragon here, I realized that it didn't matter how damned cold it was. I would kill him because I had to, to protect my mate.

Movement caught my eye as Zach dropped to the ground and started to look at the tracks in the sand. He lifted a leaf and sniffed it.

He loosened his hold and the wind took the fragile leaf from his hand, spinning the dried remnant of summer through the air before carrying it out over the water and out of sight. "Look at these tracks, they are his. In dragon form. But they don't come from or go into the water."

Well, that was the most heartening thing Zach had said the whole day.

Zach yanked me from my thoughts and from the daylight setting into darkness. "There is *no* way we're going to be able to look the whole length of Lake Michigan. There's over three hundred miles of coastline," Zach said as he looked around.

I sniffed the air and looked around for a moment before stripping off my clothes. I wrapped them up and handed them to Zach. It was freezing, the wind scraping at my human skin like ice coated in sandpaper. *I hate the cold.*

"I know. Hurry up and shift so we can end this bastard and

go home." Home. Heat. Desert. The canyonlands of Arizona where we'd been assigned once I'd grown. My egg had lain dormant for over two hundred years in the queen's true lair beneath Mt. Rainier, nourished by the pulse of Mother Earth, waiting for Zach to be born. We would claim our mate and take her home. Keep her safe. Take her often.

My cock stirred at the thought and not wanting to be any more uncomfortable than I already was, I called the magic of the Mother to me, of the elements, the ground beneath my feet, the fury of the skies and the bubbling power of the Earth's core, the molten center rose up through the ground and through my feet. It burned. It always burned, but I embraced the pain. It was a small price to pay to be reborn in my true form.

Dragon.

Power rushed through every fiber of my being and I lifted my huge head, tested the long, curved amber wings. My scales were magnificent, the color of dark whiskey or brilliant gold depending on the light.

Zach ran his hand across my golden scales, patted me on the back and jumped on, securing my clothing and shoes in a collapsible pack he removed from his pocket for this purpose. He slung the small pack over his back and settled between my shoulders. The smell of the Riven burned on the tip of my tongue, like too much burned cinnamon.

I smell his blood. And burned scales. The thought gave me great satisfaction. He was not the only dragon to draw blood this day. My body was healed, but the battle still boiled in my blood. I pointed off in the distance with the clawed tip of my wing. *His scent calls from that direction.*

The odor was overwhelming. I shook my head to get the

burning to stop. It didn't do much good, but what little it did I was grateful for. I took to the skies, following the smell through the steep bluffs and ravines that ran north along the lake where his scent simply…disappeared.

It's gone. He's gone. From what I could tell, there was no evidence of the Riven anywhere around. We landed, and Zach climbed down, looking around the area for anything that might give us a clue.

"Do you think he went into the water to throw us off his scent?"

I walked to the edge of the water and easily picked up the other dragon's scent. *Yes. He entered here.*

"He went into the water?" Zach shivered. I would have as well, however, that display of weakness was beneath me in this form. I was dragon. We feared nothing.

Apparently, he didn't stick around Lake Michigan for long, I thought to Zach.

"Why lead us all the way up here?"

I scanned the horizon, my dragon's eyes seeing for miles, the lights of Chicago a beacon in the night. *So he could hunt without interference.*

Zach turned, following my gaze and cursed. "Then we follow wherever he leads us."

Which was mostly likely to a series of half eaten human corpses, but I didn't say a word. Zach knew the cold, hard truth of a Riven as well as I did.

The sky was dark and cloudy. The thick, sticky humidity from the impending rain washed over my large amber scales. I hated the cold, the saturated feeling of standing in the humidity

—it wasn't quite as bad as diving into cold water, but still not a sensation I enjoyed.

Zach wiped at his hair, small pieces of ice falling from his head to shatter on the ground. He made his way back over to me and swung up onto my back. He'd gotten good at it over the years. He gently patted me on the neck, and I unfurled my wings. They were large, and it took some talent to jump high enough to allow my wings the acceptable room to freely move and get my thick, heavy, muscular ass into the air.

The fog grew thicker as I pressed forward into the starry dusk. I closed my large golden eyes, enjoying the feeling of being in flight—free and powerful. Relished the sensation of my wings slicing through the wind under the stars. I didn't need to use my eyes to fly, I could feel the ground beneath me and the stars above me. They were part of me as I was part of them.

I was born of the magic of Earth, created to protect this planet and every living creature upon it. Dragons had been here for millions of years, evolving as humanity did, taking on new forms. Our history was long, the memories kept in the queen's DNA and passed on to every Dragonborn to her and the king.

All life was sacred. But a Riven lost sight of that. The only thing he felt was power, the ultimate power, that of life and death. And to a Riven, humans were so deliciously terrified of going back into the arms of their mother Earth, *dust to dust*, as their churches said.

I would go gladly, if not for Zach…and the hope that my new mate might calm the fire and fury rising within me. But I didn't have much time left, and both Zach and I knew it.

One more reason to hunt this Riven and return to our mate. It was unlikely that my mother, the queen, would leave us alone for long. There was always a new threat, a new mission. Something urgent that had to be taken care of at once. The queen constantly sent all of her sons to do chores, but all fire dragons were under her command. The ice dragons answered to our father, the king, but she was still their mother. The creature we hunted now was my brother. We were all brothers. Brother hunting brother. Killing one another. Fighting for control of this world since the king had gone mad and set his ice dragons loose on the world.

King against queen. Ice against fire. The dragons had gone to war.

avo

THAT FIASCO HAD CAUSED the last human ice age in 1645, nearly four hundred years ago. And the war raged still, so many dragons and riders lost that there weren't many of us left, every unhatched egg in the queen's cave guarded like a priceless treasure.

Whenever I thought of my mother's ruby red scales, all I could think of was the fire she would bring down on us if we failed this mission. Zach and I had never failed our queen. But not out of love for her. She was as ruthless and calculating as her mate, her only true loyalty was to her sons and the planet she protected. She cared nothing for humans, tolerated the riders because her Dragonborn sons needed them, and cared little for the females we chose as mates. She was, as far as I knew, immortal, and the lives of the humans were too short for her to concern herself with. None of us knew how long she would live, and none dared ask. Theoretically, a dragon could live thousands of years…unless they were bound to a human; a dragon's healing magic significantly extended the life of their human rider and mate but shortened his own. It was a necessary exchange, and one I did not regret.

Better a couple hundred years with Zach than a thousand as a heartless monster like my parents. The current king and queen had been ruling over Earth for at least a millennium.

More than once, we'd needed to stop the queen from burning a human city to the ground, reminding her that she might be killing a future rider, or a future mate.

"Pay attention. I've got a bad feeling about this." Zach pointed to a well-lit human machine flying toward us, a small, private airplane.

My senses also picked up the scent and sound of thunderous air ahead. I snapped back to the present, the muscles in my back tightening beneath Zach's legs. After noticing the impending company, Zach tightened his thigh muscles against my back. Pivoting slightly, I banked to the right and tucked us away into a full cloud until we couldn't see the shadow any longer.

Though humans always regarded clouds as thick, fluffy puffs of entertainment—sometimes lying somewhere and staring up at them for hours on end—they were cold and wet. Regardless of the temperature, I did agree there was something magical about flying through them, especially if you were able to do it firsthand and not be secluded from their splendor inside of a flying metal deathtrap. *I don't know why humans ride in those things.*

"They're faster than walking."

Dragons are faster.

"Agreed." Zach threw his hands up into the cloud and shouted to the stars. We were heading back towards Chicago. The windy city was one of my *least* favorite places. It was quite literally everything I hated: cold and wet. Because of the water, the wind coming off the lake could be even chillier than the natural temperature of the air around us.

I couldn't stand water, not unless it came from a hot spring. After all the time we'd spent together, Zach knew that little fact about me, yet he still loved humid places. His human ancestors were from the cold northern part of Europe. Vikings and Irish poets alike. Which explained his love of whiskey, exploring, and cold, damp air.

You are a freak. I should have chosen another rider.

"Stop whining. You have an internal heater. This is fantastic. It makes me feel *alive.*"

I couldn't argue, not with his obvious joy bleeding through our telepathic link. I sighed and cranked up my internal fire. He might love the cold, but he was still small and human.

Taking advantage of the time we had left in the air, Zach leaned back on me and rested, absorbing my heat as we flew. It would take at least an hour to get back to the city, so I didn't plan to get any rest for a while yet. I could do that when we landed.

Looking ahead, the clouds took on the pink and orange shimmer of reflecting the city lights. I searched the skies, but our prey was not in the air and I feared the worst, that he was already on the ground. Hunting.

As we drew nearer and broke out of the clouds, the light

temporarily blinded me and I squinted at the city, looking for a likely place to land on the outskirts, somewhere we could escape human eyes. My wings cracked through the air as I made my way down into the smoggy city night.

Sensing the change in altitude, Zach woke up and held on as I pushed us harder and faster into the city.

I pressed into the trees and slowly lowered us to the ground next to the water, making sure there were no humans out to catch sight of us. Zach held tight to my back as I took the brunt of the landing on my large, scaled feet. Once we were safely on the ground, Zach climbed down to my wing so I could lower him safely from my back. He then stretched his legs, arching his back as he lifted his arms to stretch the rest of him.

Taking a deep breath, I lowered my head and closed my eyes, focusing on the vibrating energy circulating both around and inside of me. My entire body shook as I slowly transformed from my dragon form into my human one.

Rolling my head around for a moment as I stretched it along with the rest of my body, I held out my hand and glanced at the starry sky. It was a beautiful night. While we'd been buried in the clouds, I couldn't appreciate it as much as I would have liked because I'd needed to concentrate on hunting. But down here, on the ground, where I could see between the breaks in them and focus on their song, I sighed in momentary contentment.

Zach handed me my clothes, his brows raised. "Listening to the stars again?"

Yes.

He grinned. "A dragon poet. Sure you're not Irish?"

I ignored him and pulled on my clothing, grateful for even their small protection against the chill. Our mother told us when we were dragonlings that the stars were maps of the world put there by an ancient immortal race, our creators, protectors of all life. I had no idea if her words were true or merely fairy tales told to the young ones to make them feel special. Nor did I care. I was born of Earth, and Her magic held me, owned me. I had no desire to leave this planet and search the stars. My only desire was to find my mate and cool the fire burning inside me.

I would take Brittany in my arms and plunder her sweet mouth, learn her taste again and again as I touched every inch of her skin. Buried my fingers and my cock in her hot, wet core. Made her whimper and beg. Then I'd take her the dragon way, in her ass, filling her with dragon magic as Zach filled her with his seed, bonding her to us and creating a new life, a new member of the Dragonborn. Son or daughter made no difference to me. Dragonborn were special gifts, male and female. And Brittany. Mother help me, I could still taste her on my tongue. Could hardly think. I didn't want to hunt. I *needed*. Her. Only her.

"First we hunt. Then we fuck. Stay with me." Zach slapped me on the back and tossed my boots at my feet.

As a heavy sigh escaped me, I rubbed my tired hands through my long, blond hair. The wind chilled me once again. No one had warned me of the intense pain that came along with being in a squishy human form, and sure as hell, no one told me about being able to burn in the damn sun. The first time I'd allowed my human flesh to burn in the sun, I thought I was going to die. The more I thought about it, the more it baffled me. Did humans actually *cook?* Is that why they burned? Did the sun *cook* their flesh?

According to dragon lore, many humans had died a fiery death, not from the sun, but from dragons. At one time, the Dragonborn had nearly hunted humans to extinction. The queen normally refused to speak of those dark days. According to her, it was like hell on earth. Dragons had ruled the world, and humans were our main source of food. I didn't pay enough attention in history lessons to remember exactly when we were first forbidden to eat humans. The only thing I *did* know was that it was way before I came into this damned world. And that the binding between dragon and rider had been one of the reasons the dark times ended.

Zach's voice broke me from my reverie as he reached into a trash bin along the sidewalk and pulled out an abandoned newspaper. "What the hell?"

Who still reads the newspaper? Don't these humans have smartphones?

Zach frowned, scanning the headline. "You don't."

I am a dragon.

"Well, you aren't the only one in Chicago." He held out the paper and I read the headline. *26 Dead. Serial Killer Strikes Again.*

Damn it. The Riven was definitely hunting here. I read the details, the bodies found torn in pieces, organs missing, and the victims scattered along the water's edge, all within a thirty-mile radius.

The police had no clues, no suspects.

The public was panicked, avoiding the lake and parks all over the city.

The mayor was considering a curfew until the killer was caught.

He is hunting here. He will have a den nearby. With a Riven in Chicago, the last thing we needed was for me to be seen in my dragon form. No one would ever be caught by the human authorities. This was dragon business, and we took care of our own problems. A dragon who had lost control could do a lot of damage in a small amount of time, especially when it came to the humans.

"Do you still have his scent?" Zach asked, staring at the dark shadows among the trees lining the edge of the water.

Of course. It was late, but there were hours left until most humans would be sleeping in their beds. The Riven would be hunting. And so would we.

~

Zach

THE HUNT PROVED FRUITLESS, the Riven untraceable. Twilight had faded to darkness and the hunger to be with our mate, to protect her, fuck her, sleep with her safely between us, was strong. Iavo, especially, refused to wait to find her. He was obsessed. On edge. I'd never seen him like this and for the first time since we'd been bonded as dragon and rider, I was afraid. Afraid of what would happen to Iavo if Brittany refused us, refused his mating bond, his claim.

I wasn't sure where to begin our search, but Iavo tracked her easily. He followed her scent to a small dorm room at the university. When we knocked, a fragile human male answered. Too thin, blood polluted with drugs, he looked sickly. Weak. And he was home alone.

"Hey, dudes."

Dudes? Iavo rolled his eyes and walked away, his elite dragon senses unwilling to endure the stench of the strange smoke that wafted into the hall. "We are looking for Brittany. She stopped by here earlier today, looking for her brother?" There was no way this man was related to our mate.

His blood did not sing to me. I glanced to Iavo, the question in my eyes. A dragon could always sense a Dragonborn, the magic in their blood.

I almost sighed with relief when Iavo confirmed my instincts. This man was not Brittany's brother and, therefore, not ours.

"Look, man, she stopped by this morning. Garrett ain't here and I told her that when she came back this afternoon. He shacks up with his girlfriend a lot, you know?"

"I wonder why." Peering past the man's shoulder I saw a pigsty of leftover pizza, beer cans and drug paraphernalia scattered on the floor surrounded by dirty clothing. This weakling wasn't related to Brittany, but his roommate was, in fact, the brother she'd been searching for, Garrett.

"And where might we find his girlfriend?" I asked.

He shrugged, unconcerned. "Not his keeper, dude. I have no idea. Don't even really like the guy, you know."

Turning on my heel, I left without another word. None was needed. Iavo fell into step beside me as we made our way down the stairs. "He said she was here this afternoon. Can you pick up her trail outside?"

Of course.

Half an hour later, Lake Michigan looked like glass as Iavo and I walked up the navy pier towards the only seafood restaurant there. The same place we'd first met her. Brittany mentioned her job last night. I knew we should leave her alone, let her work in peace, but neither Iavo nor I could get her out of our heads.

When we walked through the front door, the hostess looked us up and down as if we were eye candy. "Can I help you?" the bubbly blonde hostess asked with a toothy, white smile.

"Yes, we need to see Brittany, can you tell her Zach and Iavo are here?" I said casually.

The blonde nodded her head and walked off to find Brittany. It wasn't long before she appeared from around a corner. Her blonde hair was perfectly done, her makeup was artfully applied, and her piercing blue eyes made me forget to breathe.

And you accuse me of thinking with my cock. Iavo's telepathic voice was full of laughter.

"Shut up." I mouthed the words through my smile as she came up to us with a look of curiosity written all over her beautiful face.

"What's up, guys? I'm not supposed to have visitors. I'm going to get in trouble if we don't make this quick," Brittany said as she walked us out onto the empty patio.

"We stopped by your brother's dorm, and his roommate said he was with his girlfriend. He's fine and should be back tomorrow. Garrett's sickly roommate said there wasn't anything to worry about," I said as I put my hand against Brittany's lower back. Iavo closed the gap, as Brittany backed up with her brow furrowed.

Her eyes briefly widened as she looked from me to Iavo and then back again. Then, they narrowed, and her brows furrowed. She'd gone from obvious shock or even fear to pissed off in no time flat. "No one asked you to check in on my brother. I can take care of this myself," Brittany said with an indignant tone.

My smile faded as I attempted to reassure her. "You said you were worried about your brother, so we checked in on him. We are yours now, Brittany. We will always take care of you and didn't want you to worry."

Careful, Zach, her heart is beating too quickly and she smells of rage. You are making her angry.

"Shut up, Iavo. I've got this."

"Shut up?" Brittany's gaze darted over her shoulder, to Iavo, standing silent, as always, at her back, before looking back to me. "He didn't say anything."

I sighed. There was so much to tell her. So much to teach her. It was too easy to forget that she wasn't part of our world. Not yet.

I took her hands in mine and Iavo's palms landed on her shoulders. We held her between us. "Brittany, we are here on a mission. Once that mission is complete, we must return to our home. To Arizona."

"You're leaving? When? Now?"

"No. As soon as we complete the hunt, and we want you to come with us," I said still holding that smile. Hoping. Praying.

"Hunt?" Trying to take another step back, Brittany bumped into Iavo's chest, shook her head and responded, "I can't go anywhere. I don't even know where my brother is, and after our separation as children, I'm not about to go off to Arizona and leave him."

Iavo started yelling in my head, *The Riven's not far from here, and we're about to be in way over our fucking heads if we don't get out of here. The last thing we need is him catching her scent and going after our mate.*

"Duty calls, Brittany. Please, think about our offer. We will return when we have finished our…business here."

Iavo stepped out from behind her and walked to the edge of the pier. He was barely holding back his beast, his skin swirling with the amber color of his dragon as he held off the change. *Hurry, Zach. He is close.*

Lifting my hand to caress our mate's soft cheek, I leaned in and kissed her on the forehead. "Stay inside, okay? Promise me. It's not safe. We'll be back as soon as we can."

"Duty calls? Or hunting?" Brittany crossed her arms and waited for an answer, which I did not feel the need to provide. After several long minutes, she regarded us carefully before simply nodding at us and walking back into the relative safety of the restaurant. Iavo turned to face me, his eyes glowing with his power.

She's going to be a target now. He's close, really fucking close. I need to kill him. Now.

He was right, and I knew it. If we didn't move quickly, we would become the hunted and so would Brittany. We couldn't let that happen, not when we had just found her.

CHAPTER 6

rittany

WELL, that little visit had been more than unexpected. It felt—strange. Inside, I was screaming for joy, drawn to them. Part of me wanted to yell at them to come back and take me with them. It was hard to explain why I felt so close to them, needful of them, but I did. Their presence made me feel safe in a way I never had before, but there was my brain arguing with my heart, insisting that something was *off*. That Zach and Iavo were keeping secrets. Big ones.

Why was Iavo mute? And if he was really mute, why did Zach talk to him like he wasn't? And what were they hunting? Zach had said the word 'hunt' multiple times. Hunt. And Mission. And yours? Zach said *they* were mine. *They?*

I wondered what Iavo thought about that little statement.

Seemed Zach had a habit of talking for both of them, which was beginning to annoy me. Was Iavo too stupid to use sign language? To learn how to read or write? Hell, he could try charades for all I cared.

And they were mine? Mine?

After one night? Even I wasn't that foolish, no matter how high I still was from the orgasm induced stupor. How could they be mine when I had no idea who they were?

My imagination filled in all the blanks. Spies. CIA. Mafia. Hitmen. Super warriors who were part of some uber-top-secret government program like I saw on my favorite television shows.

Logically, I knew I had just met then, knew almost nothing about them, and shouldn't have wanted to go anywhere with them, let alone out of town. I realized just how strange it was for them to track down my brother to try to talk to him, and it was just as strange for them to come to my place of business. It was kind of creepy and stalkerish—but my heart and instincts refused to let that take hold.

They were safe. They were mine. And my logical brain could scream all it wanted to, the rest of me wasn't listening.

I felt like I was left in a daydream when the twins left, a mix of emotions tearing at me. My shift seemed to drag on like it never wanted to end. Even worse was that the hours always seemed to drag on weekdays anyway. Business was always a bit slower—especially late at night when everyone was more than likely at home, reading bedtime stories to their kids and watching sitcoms. The slow pace did nothing to allow me to get lost in work and forget the passage of time. Apparently, there weren't as many drunk people on weekdays.

Once the weekend came, people packed the place and the alcohol flowed. From morning mimosas to the whiskey chasers, beers to shots, we were hopping all day and into the evening. It kept me constantly busy, and I had no time to watch the clock.

The tips were always best on the weekends. That was more than likely because most of my customers were men, and they tended to get a bit gracious once they'd had a few. Most of the time, they kept their thoughts—and their hands—to themselves, so it didn't bother me much.

But tonight was different. It was slow and boring. Tonight felt like it dragged out from beginning to end. With the twins on my mind, it was even worse. I had a customer curse me out because the cook couldn't make her scallops right—as if that was my fault. I didn't cook it, lady. Three plates, forty minutes, and three fails later, she left without leaving me one dime for a tip.

I think she might just have been my worst customer to date.

In addition to her, I had one customer seated in my section. He wasn't rude or annoying like Ms. Scallops had been. Though, that wasn't to say I enjoyed having him. He registered on the weirdo radar. He was a handsome, tall, blond man with golden eyes. He didn't talk. I wasn't sure if he was sick, or if he was mute, but he was certainly quiet. The man sat there jittery and constantly looking over his shoulder as I went to the serving station to get his drink, Scotch on the rocks.

His gaze followed me as I worked my way around the tables, the interest in his eyes not the hot and sexy kind. More like the *I-am-thinking-about-dissecting-you* kind. I had no reason to think that way, but there was just something about him that made my skin tingle with alarm, not lust.

I whispered to Lucy. "Man, I hope he's an eat and go kind of guy. He gives me the creeps. There's something about him that just feels… off."

Lucy snuck a peek around the corner. "Yeah, I can see it. He looks like a tweaker. See how twitchy he is? Probably an addict…or a dealer." She shrugged. "Hot, but definitely creepy."

Her face screwed up a bit as she looked him over for a few seconds. Then, she shook her head and turned to rush off to the hostess station to welcome the new customers. Lucy was the perfect hostess, she was beautiful, personable, outgoing, and just the right amount of confident without looking like a complete snob.

Mentally, I prepared myself to go back to the creepy-guy table before walking over. As usual, I pasted on a smile—even if I didn't quite mean it. I set the drink down in front of him and pulled out my pen and pad of paper.

"I'm ready for your order if you've made a decision," I said with a smile.

He picked up the menu and pointed at the shrimp scampi. Mute? Right. Another one. Like that was totally normal.

"That's a great choice," I said. "One of my favorites. We'll have it right out." I put my order pad away and flashed another smile. When I reached for his menu, he grabbed my wrist, not painfully, but hard enough that I knew I couldn't pull away.

"Hey!" I yanked on my wrist but he just held it and stared for a few seconds. When I realized he wasn't going to do anything else, and I was surrounded by a roomful of people, I calmed down and gave him my very best version of a death glare. "Let. Me. Go."

His blazing yellow eyes blinked slowly, almost like a lazy

snake basking in the sun, and he leaned down over my hand and *sniffed.*

What the hell?

I yanked harder this time, ready to put up a fight if he didn't let me go, but he released me, sat back in the booth and smirked like he knew something I didn't. The edgy nerves he'd been displaying, the bouncing knee, the constant looking over his shoulder, the twitching…all gone. In their place was complete calm, as if suddenly he had the answers to everything in the universe.

I took a step back. Two. His eyes had changed somehow, they seemed brighter, and he looked at me again, but this time it was different. It was like he was taking inventory. He stared. At everything. Shoes. Knees. Clothing. Even my ears. When he looked me in the eye at last, I was shaking.

He noticed, glancing at my hand as the pen I'd been holding rattled against the order pad in the pocket of my apron. My reaction made him smile.

This was serial killer weird. He'd just gone from creepy to terrifying in the space of a few seconds.

I turned on my heel and walked away as if nothing had happened. Once I was out of the dining area, I hid in the hall between the kitchen and bussers' station. I couldn't wait for that guy to leave. Something was really, really wrong with him. Lucy thought he was on drugs, but I'd seen enough of that growing up to know that wasn't his problem.

This one reeked of sociopath. Killer.

A wolf in sheep's clothing. He was perfect. Sexy. His chest was muscular and filled out his t-shirt to perfection. His gaze was intensely golden, just like Iavo's. I'd never seen eyes like that before, and now there were two of them? And, like Iavo, he didn't talk?

But that wasn't what had me shaking, hiding in the hall like a coward.

I didn't want to bring his food to him, so I had a bus boy drop it off as I got a drink of water in the kitchen and made my way to the balcony out back to get some fresh air. It helped, but not as much as I'd hoped. I focused on the breeze blowing in over the water and the way the moonlight lit the clouds. It was peaceful out here. Quiet.

I bent forward with my hands on the railing as I tried to stop the wave of nausea that had taken me over.

Deep breath, Brittany, deep breath, Brittany, I kept thinking to myself, hoping the words would keep me centered so I didn't throw up everywhere.

When I was young and in the foster system, I had several breakdowns. As a result, I learned how to self-soothe. I learned what to say to myself to calm down. For me, all it took was telling myself to breathe.

I grabbed Lucy, who finished up with Mr. Creepy. We did that for each other, stepping in and taking over when things got weird. Which was more often than I liked.

When they were both gone, I worked like a zombie through the rest of my shift. All I could think about was the guys. Zach and Iavo. No matter what I tried to focus on, they weren't ever far behind. My obsession seemed strange to me, but I'd never been in love before, so maybe this was what falling in love felt like.

But with two of them?

I wasn't sure what the rest of the world would have to say

about that, but I couldn't change it now. Zach was funny and gentle and playful. Patient. But Iavo? For someone who didn't talk, he communicated just fine. Those eyes spoke a thousand words and I knew what he wanted without being told. When he touched me, I knew. When his eyes burned into me like I was the most beautiful, desirable woman in the world, I knew. His intensity was impossible to resist. But Zach's gentleness with me, the way he liked to play? I needed that, too.

It wasn't just lust. One night together and I was analyzing them both like they were my own personal jigsaw puzzle, and I couldn't wait to be snapped into place between them again.

The butterflies in my stomach gave way to heat. My cheeks always betrayed me, and I blushed when they came to mind. Lucy, the hostess, kept teasing me. She had noticed my flushed cheeks from the moment the guys had walked in. It was kind of hard to deny, especially with how flustered I had become when they had come in to check up on me. Kind of sweet. Annoying, in an alpha male way, but I had to admit that it made me feel special. Like they cared. And everything inside me craved that feeling.

"Come on, Britt. Let's get off our feet." Lucy pulled me along outside, carrying a bottle of wine and two glasses. Two steaming plates were up on the counter as we passed. I yelled thanks to the cooks and we headed outside for a few minutes to rest and eat. We'd catch up on our work. The back of house always took longer to close up than we did.

The darkness always engulfed us when we were on the pier. With no light pollution coming from the lake, I knew the restaurant looked like a beacon on the end of the pier. The night sky seemed infinitely darker, and some sailors said we looked like a lighthouse jutting out into the water.

With the gentle waves of the tide rolling in and the soft breeze, I let out a heavy sigh, feeling a bit more content. I stood on the balcony and enjoyed the moment of quiet. My feet throbbed, my lower back ached, and I smelled like fried food and grease.

Gross.

A breeze from the open lake brushed a strand of hair across my cheek, but I didn't mind. It felt amazing as I watched stars melt into the darkness. This was my favorite time of day.

Lucy handed me a glass of white wine. I grabbed it with both hands, smelled it, then took that first sip. "Thank you," I said as I smiled at Lucy.

Lucy just smiled and nodded as she tipped up her own glass. Lucy and I were the ones closing the front of the house, and I didn't mind that at all. She could definitely be fun to work with, especially when we were bored and needed to keep things entertaining to pass the time.

Lucy locked the door behind us as we made our way back inside. I grabbed our wrapped plates of fish and chips and she grabbed the wine. By the time Lucy made it back inside to the table, I had already gotten them ready, and put the malt vinegar down between us.

I mean, come on. You can't have fish and chips without malt vinegar.

Everything was quiet as we sat and ate and chatted.

"We can't have dinner without at least one toast. Right? I toast to the extremely sexy man-meat you have chasing after you. I'll take the leftovers," Lucy said with a smile as she sipped her wine and giggled.

I laughed nervously, coughing a couple of times to clear my throat before nodding and lifting my glass, a large smile still on my face. "I'll drink to sexy men." We both tipped the glasses back and drank before setting them back on the table. "But there won't be any leftovers," I said as I giggled and took another sip. I could feel a slight warmth as I finished off my glass of wine and welcomed the feeling.

Lucy nodded and finished her glass as well. "Damn. I was holding out hope, but I don't blame you."

We both stood and had the place cleaned up and closed down in no time. I hurried. I would admit it. Although I did ignore Lucy's knowing grins the rest of the night. Were two men two much?

I'm sure plenty of conservative ladies would roll over in their graves, but the thought of turning away either Zach or Iavo didn't feel right. They were connected somehow. Not one man to love, but two halves of the same whole. I didn't understand the feeling, but in my heart, I knew it was right.

"See you tomorrow night. Have fun," Lucy said as I walked her to her car. I nodded and walked farther out into the lot as she started her car and drove away. The pier was always quiet at this time of night. Except the occasional weekend when there were drunks out, I found it to be quite peaceful. Taking advantage of the tranquility, I took a walk along the pier and even stopped to look out at the beautiful dark water. I imagined what it must be like to just get on a boat and go. Not look back, not worry about everyday things, not worry about work the next day. Just go. Maybe one day I'd have that.

But that day was not today.

I was tired and I had just worked a very long shift. My feet were hurting, but that was kind of my fault because I'd forgotten my good shoes when I left for work. Tomorrow would be a better day. I knew it. And tomorrow, I'd get to see my brother. I was determined. I'd stalk him if I had to.

Thinking about the next day also brought with it the hope that I would get to see the twins again. I liked being around them, even though they were just a little strange. It occurred to me that they couldn't have been as close as they were without knowing they were kind of strange already. I wondered if it was completely normal—normal to *them* anyway—to share a woman the way they did.

I'd never come across men like them before, but maybe that was the point. Strange as it was, I couldn't stop thinking about them, and it was more than the crazy effect they had on my hormones. A lot more.

I *missed* them.

I wanted to be near them. They made me feel safe and beautiful and part of a real family. I felt like I belonged with them, and that was something I hadn't felt since I'd been a kid struggling to take care of my little brother.

Regardless, I couldn't allow my libido to distract me. There were a lot of things in my life that I needed to sort before I tried to sort this one. The fact that I'd accidentally fallen for two men wasn't lost on me. I just refused to read into it any more than I already had. I had a plan. I had to reconnect with my brother. Dating was pretty far down my priority list.

Still… That didn't mean I would turn down an opportunity to be with them again.

The quiet lapping sound of water hitting the rocks normally made me feel dreamy and content. I could listen to the sound for hours. But tonight, the darkness seemed to press in on me, making it hard to breathe. It felt like the darkness had eyes. So I hastened my journey down the stairs to the large parking lot. Even then, the familiar safety of being on solid ground, of the pavement beneath my feet, did nothing to help. Instead, the moment I stepped foot on the blacktop, I a strange feeling came over me.

No one's here; it's all in your head. No one's here, it's just quiet. No one's following you; it's all in your head.

Over and over, I repeated the reassurance as I rushed through the large, open lot. I walked in and out of the shadows cast by the parking lot's light poles as I made my way across the lot that had been full of cars all day long. There were a few scattered cars left, but not many. There weren't many places for someone to hide at night. But I felt open. Exposed.

Like I had a target on my back and a sniper was waiting to pull the trigger. Which was paranoid. And stupid. I was a big fat nobody. No one had ever cared where I was or what I was doing. As far as I knew—other than my run-in with the super-sexy twins –nothing had changed.

My eyes darted left to right, looking for something, anything that would make me so uneasy. But still, I saw nothing. I finally tried to relax. "Stupid, overactive imagination."

Just as reached my run-down car, I felt a tingle on the back of my neck. A small jolt of electricity rocketed up my spine and goose bumps prickled across my skin—as if my body was trying to warn me.

Too late.

I turned just in time to see a blur of green. The world around me spun then as I went airborne, going higher and higher into the sky. I screamed and twisted, fighting whatever had ahold of me, but to no avail. No one was listening. I couldn't see anything; everything was whipping around me, and I couldn't focus. Nothing made any sense, and I still had no idea how I became airborne.

∿

Zach

LOOKING over my shoulder several times, I checked to make sure no one saw as I jumped and landed with a quick thud on Iavo's golden amber scales. We'd been hunting for hours, the Riven's scent leading us in circles.

He was toying with us. Intelligent. Still in control. Unlike the last few Riven we'd hunted. They had been lost to the killing madness. Reckless and easy to track down.

This one was different. I knew Iavo felt it as well. He'd pushed both of us to the brink of collapse, refusing to stop, to give up the hunt.

With only a few powerful movements, Iavo pushed off and his wings propelled us forward into the dark night sky, straight up, flying high into the cover of the thick clouds.

He's killed again. I taste blood in the wind.

As he banked to the right, I held on with my strong leg muscles. As a rider, it was easy to get stronger and stronger. I learned to use my entire body—especially my legs and core—to balance and hold on to the back of a speeding dragon. Battles were even more intense, but we'd learned early to work together. Sitting on his back was natural to me now, and to him? I was another weapon, a means for him to attack from his back and not just his mouth, tail and claws.

We landed in the dark on the bluffs along the side of the lake. There were no lights here, but a small group of shops was close. Iavo was right; I could hear a scream coming from just over the hill. I jumped from Iavo's back and rushed up and over the horizon as he took to the air above me, ready for battle.

As I cleared the rise, I saw the dragon. Larger than Iavo, he was a dark, magnificent green and for a moment I was paralyzed at the idea of killing something so beautiful.

The screaming of the woman trapped under his claws snapped me out of it and I ran toward the dragon, knowing I would be too late to save her.

We knew he was going to leave a trail of bodies behind him, but I didn't expect to get a ringside seat to one of his kills.

I cleared the long, grassy knoll in under a minute. Chills ran through me as I heard the woman calling out for help. The Riven raised his long snout into the air and roared a challenge to Iavo. The green monster seemed to feed on her fear, as if the tiny, squirming human he tortured entranced him.

I wasn't fooled and knew Iavo would not take the bait either. The dragon wasn't toying with the woman; he was toying with *us.*

As if the beast could read my thoughts, he turned his head so that his huge eye looked right at me as he dug his long claw deeper into her thigh and started to drag her across the park with him.

Unable to attack outright for fear of injuring the woman, Iavo landed a few feet away from the other dragon and the two beasts circled one another like wrestlers on the matt. Instead of attacking Iavo, as I expected, the Riven narrowed his large, amber eyes and lifted the woman in his claws up to his mouth, gripping her tightly in his teeth.

Her screaming silenced as the green dragon's large jaws closed over the small body. Iavo and I stopped in our tracks. We were too late. We couldn't save her. I could feel through the bond Iavo and I shared just how pissed off that had made my dragon. He took the human's death as a failure. And Iavo never failed his queen. Never.

Stay back! Iavo shouted in my mind as he lunged at the beast. Now that his hostage was dead, there was nothing stopping my dragon from striking at the Riven's heart.

The green dragon lowered his head and met Iavo's charge head on. Giant maws clashed, a mixed eruption of fire and ice blasting into the sky above them as they battled to destroy one another.

Gold and green, the two beasts battered and clawed at each other. Iavo took a hit to his back from the green dragon's tail but scored with a swipe of his claws across our enemy's chest.

Payback, asshole.

"Stop playing around and kill him." I pulled the revolver I carried from the inside of my jacket and waited. The .357 was a last line of defense. I couldn't easily hide anything larger when we were out in public. Unfortunately, it wouldn't do much more than slow down the green dragon or piss him off. But it had saved my ass before, given Iavo the few seconds he needed to recover from a hit.

Besides, I felt like an old-fashioned cowboy when I pulled the long, steel barrel out into the moonlight. Which was my own personal secret, and one I never shared with my dragon.

I know about your little silver weapon, cowboy. *You forget you have no secrets from me.*

"Just hurry up. I want—" I stopped midsentence, unwilling to give the green dragon any information that might hurt us… or *her.* But the truth was that I was as hungry for our woman as my dragon had ever been. She was in my blood now. All I could think about. And I wanted to get this job done and get back to her. Strip her naked. Make her come over and over on my tongue as Iavo fucked her from behind.

I know what you want. Iavo sent me an image of our mate sprawled between us in the bed, her head thrown back, her skin glistening with pleasure.

Yes. That was exactly what I wanted.

The Riven grunted loudly, flapped his large wings and took to the sky. Iavo bunched his legs to give chase but froze with a roar.

Pain lanced through me. Not physical and not my own.

Iavo's. I knew that dragons could communicate with one another on some kind of common mental path, but I wasn't able to hear all of them. Only Iavo, through the bond we shared.

"What happened?" I yelled at Iavo as the green dragon flew just out of striking distance and landed, as if watching a show.

Brittany. He found Brittany. I can smell her blood.

I expected Iavo to attack. The Riven to run.

But the evil bastard didn't run.

He laughed.

rittany

EVERYTHING SPUN AGAIN as if I had just been thrown into the air. I landed with a loud *thud* on the concrete, my head hitting so hard I saw stars. I rolled several times before coming to an agonizing stop. Excruciating pain radiated through my body and head, but the worse of it radiated from my leg.

I tried to move, to examine my leg, hoping for the best but not expecting it at that point.

The scream that left my throat was not voluntary and I knew the large bone in my thigh was broken. Fighting not to pass out, I screamed into the darkness. "You asshole!" I had no idea who…or what…I was screaming at, but I knew he could hear me. I somehow *knew.*

I laid down and tried to catch my breath, but it came in

short, uneven spasms. I had to get out of the open, find cover. Call 9-1-1. Something. I was *not* going to just lay down and die. That wasn't me.

Just breathe!

My head pounded, and my vision was blurry. Reaching up with trembling hands, I winced when I touched the back of my skull. The swelling was significant, the size of a golf ball and growing as I laid there and tried to remain as small and quiet as possible.

Rolling onto my stomach, I used my arms to drag myself toward the nearest vehicle. It was a black pickup with jacked up wheels, but it was cover.

Gritting my teeth against the pain I pulled myself forward on my elbows. The new position seemed to help my vision clear and I stopped moving as the figure of a man came closer.

Relief flooded me until I looked up and saw his face. He was the creepy, hand sniffer from earlier. The one who couldn't talk. He'd only pointed at everything he'd wanted. The one whose eyes had made me feel like a mouse caught in a trap.

He reached for me, his rough hands poking at the back of my head with no gentleness or mercy. When he pulled his fingers back, fresh blood dripped from the tips. With a grin that nearly made me vomit, he lifted the blood to his mouth and licked them clean.

"Who are you? What do you want?" I asked.

He placed his finger over his lips to silence me and shook his head in warning for me to be quiet. The creep factor was off the charts now, and I realized I was probably going to die. He was the serial killer the police had been tracking. He had to be. He totally fit the serial killer profile. White male. In his thirties?

Sociopath. He'd probably started torturing animals when he was in pre-school.

I couldn't run. Couldn't fight. Not physically. So I did the only thing I could. I glared. "Fuck you."

He didn't react, which was a relief and terrifying all at the same time. He was like a robot, completely lacking in a normal human response.

Shock was setting in. I was cold. Too cold. My entire body began to shake uncontrollably.

He noticed. Smiled. Ran the back of his fingers along my cheek in a bizarre caress.

"What do you want from me?"

In silence, he stood and stepped back, holding my gaze as if commanding me to watch. I couldn't look away, refused to turn my back on the threat, but what I saw made me think I must have hit my head a *lot* harder than I thought.

His body began to twitch and he dropped to all fours, his eyes glowing so brightly they lit up the dark pavement surrounding us. The air changed, sparked with electricity or...I didn't know what. I'd never felt anything like it.

Or had I? The tingling along my skin, the pressure building in the air, it was like something was about to happen.

And then, it did.

Staring at him, studying him as I tried to absorb the truth of the madness, I saw him transform. Right before my eyes, this handsome, tall, blond-haired, green-eyed *man* transformed from a human being into the impossible. He'd changed into a large, green, and iridescent *dragon* the size of a small aircraft. Maybe a bull elephant with wings? He was huge.

His scales sparkled like emeralds in sunlight. His claws were a dark, earthy brown as long as my arm. Sharp. Long. His eyes glowed yellow, as if lit from within. And his teeth looked like something I'd only ever seen in the museums that displayed extinct dinosaur bones.

T-Rex had nothing on this thing.

He was scary as hell.

And so beautiful he nearly took my breath away. The very sight of him seemed impossible, but there he was. My eyes darted upward as he pulled back into the air and breathed large shards of ice onto the ground surrounding me, creating a lake of ice out of the pavement as he closed me in. I rolled under the truck but got caught in the forearm by a jagged shard of ice. The extreme cold burned as it pierced through my skin like a needle.

I didn't want to give the bastard any more satisfaction, but I screamed. The ice made my arm feel like it was being cut in two as I held the wound to my chest to stop the bleeding.

My head was bleeding. I had a gaping wound from a seven-inch piece of ice that had stabbed into my damned arm. Why was he coming after me?

Or maybe he had been following me for quite some time… I remembered the feeling that had come over me the other day in the park. Had he been watching me then?

Was I being hunted by a *dragon?*

My laugh was filled with hysteria and pain even though I found nothing about the situation funny or amusing. I suppose it was a defense mechanism over the absolute mind-blowing situation I found myself in. Noises surrounding me pulled me from my cluttered and broken thoughts. I turned my head, looking in all directions as I tried to see what was happening. Where the monster was.

I had to be hallucinating, didn't I? Had someone at the bar slipped something into one of my drinks? Was I tripping?

Maybe. But the ice was real, making the normally cool air icy cold as it swirled around me under the truck. I should have been freezing, but I felt warm. Numb. Blood pooled under me as it soaked into my clothing. My eyes stung as tears tried to form but I didn't have the energy to blink or fight them off, so they rolled down my temples, freezing in the hair above my ears.

I was dying. Alone. And the dragon—or whatever he was—was gone. Silence surrounded me as I reached for the cell phone still, by some miracle, in my pocket. I fumbled to unlock the screen, to call someone, anyone, for help.

 *ach*

IAVO IGNORED the Riven and I followed his lead as he bent a shoulder, indicating I should climb up at once. The moment I was settled, Iavo leaped into the air, flying at top speed back the way we had come. Back to the restaurant on the pier where we'd checked in on her a few hours ago.

I still had no idea what the Riven had said to him, but Iavo's entire being focused on finding Brittany. His emotions were in total lockdown. Ice cold. After the initial burst of agony from him, I felt nothing. Emptiness.

As if we'd already lost her.

I refused to think about that possibility as Iavo raced back to the city.

Iavo roared when we were still a good distance away. *I smell her blood, Zach.* His emotions blasted through me and I gasped. Rage. A killing rage.

He was close to splintering. Too close. "She's not dead. Keep yourself together. She might need you." I ignored the unspoken understanding that flowed between us. Iavo was close to losing control, to giving in to the darkness. He was close to becoming what we hunted.

If we lost Brittany, there would be no stopping him. He'd kill me first. Most Riven murdered their riders before beginning their rampage through the rest of the human population.

We broke through a cloud and it was my turn to fear the worst. The parking lot was covered in emergency vehicles. An ambulance was parked on a sea of ice, our mate strapped to a bed as they loaded her unmoving form inside.

"Stay out of sight, Iavo. We need to follow them. Find out where they take her."

Iavo grunted and we waited, ignoring the police officers, the dozen other humans walking around the crime scene with cameras and evidence bags. I didn't care about any of it. Only her.

The ambulance sped away and we followed from the air to a trauma hospital with a helicopter landing pad on the roof. Iavo landed there and I slid off his back, throwing the satchel of clothing I carried for him in his direction as I took off at a run. "Get dressed. I'll find her."

If we didn't act—and fast—there was no doubt in my mind that she would dead, and very soon.

The elevator took me straight to the emergency triage area and I heard the sound of doctors and nurses scrambling.

"Brittany? Brittany, can you hear me?"

The sound of my mate's cry of pain nearly made me collapse with relief and I stumbled toward the sound. A thin sheet had been pulled around the bed where they held her, and people were scrambling in and out of the space in a mix of organized chaos.

"Brittany? This is Doctor Wethers. Can you hear me?"

"Doctor?" Her whisper was weak, confused, but alive. She was alive.

"We need to get a splint on that arm. We've given you something for the pain, but I need to examine your arm and your leg. Okay? It's going to hurt. I'm sorry. We have to move your arm and your leg to make sure you can get through the CT."

"CT?"

"Does your head hurt? Can you see me? How many fingers am I holding up? Brittany? Stay with me. How many fingers do you see?"

"Two….Three…One." I had to strain to hear her voice.

"Good job. We're going to stabilize you and get a CT of your head to check things out, okay? I've got the orthopedic docs on the way to take care of your leg and your arm. Hang in there. We're going to take care of you."

She cried out as the nursing team adjusted her position. I heard the rustling and the doctor walked out into the main area less than a minute later, motioning for a nurse to come over.

"We need ortho. Tell them we've got a distal femur fracture and a large puncture wound with a nightstick fracture in the left arm. We're stabilizing the patient, waiting for a CT of the head, but the femur will need to be dealt with as soon as possible. I'm worried about the bleeding. She could be headed for compartment syndrome. Call neuro and tell them to get their on-call down here. She'd got a pretty significant head injury. Prep surgery and call anesthesia. They're not going to be able to wait."

"Yes, Doctor." I heard the nurse, but my brain was trying to process everything they'd just said.

The doctor looked up and saw me standing there. "Can I help you? You're not supposed to be back here." He had intelligent eyes, sharp but kind. He looked like he was about forty years old and I was relieved that Brittany wasn't in the hands of a first-year resident.

"I'm here for Brittany."

His gaze darted to my left hand, which I'd anticipated and kept just out of sight. "And are you a relative?"

"I'm her husband." She was mine, and I made sure it showed in my gaze. The doctor nodded.

"How much of that did you hear?"

"All of it."

He nodded again and motioned for a nurse who was walking by. "This is Brittany's husband. Take care of him for me?"

"Okay, sure." The young man smiled up at me. "Come with me. We'll get some paperwork filled out and then we'll find out what's going on."

Paperwork? No. Brittany was hurt, badly. She needed Iavo. I believed the doctors and nurses could save her, but she'd be in too much pain. Would take too long to heal. She would suffer because we had failed to protect her and that was not acceptable.

Just as I was about to protest, the elevator opened behind

me and I knew it was Iavo by the confused look on the doctor's face.

Where is she? Iavo's voice filled my head like a shout but no one around us reacted. Iavo was using dragon magic to turn their attention away from him. He wasn't invisible, exactly. He just had a way of making sure people didn't notice him.

"So, how long will Brittany be in there?" I asked the doctor, but pointed to the curtain surrounding her, the stream of people walking in and out, for Iavo's benefit.

"As soon as she's stable, we'll take her to radiology for that CT."

I nodded. "So, she has a broken leg, broken arm and a head injury. You think she needs surgery."

No. She is mine. I will heal her. Keep the others away.

The doctor sighed. "We don't know anything for sure. We're running a few tests. I'll have more answers for you soon. We're taking good care of her."

"Can I see her?"

He shook his head and the nurse took me by the elbow. "Not yet. You'd be in the way and we're getting ready to take her to radiology. As soon as she's stabilized, you'll be the first to know."

I allowed the nurse to lead me away, but I was stalling, giving Iavo a bit of help distracting the others. I felt Iavo walk by, saw him enter the space, careful to dodge any humans in his way. He could escape notice, but not if one of them ran straight into him.

When Iavo disappeared behind the curtain, I breathed a sigh of relief and followed the nurse to the admissions station. I gave Brittany my last name and the insurance the Dragonborn used when necessary. The shell corporation owned by the queen and her dragons had served us well through the years. We were wealthy beyond belief, with all the benefits, weapons and homes we needed to do our job protecting the planet, and humanity, from the king's insanity and the ice dragons forced to do his bidding. The health insurance was rarely used, as dragon magic could heal almost anything, but the insurance was never turned down. We had a no questions asked policy that the queen herself had negotiated years ago. Dragonborn were precious, and there wasn't always a spare dragon around when someone got hurt.

I filled out paperwork and paced in the waiting room, drinking bad coffee.

Where the hell was Iavo? And what was taking so long?

Iavo

SHE LOOKED SO FRAGILE, so delicate swallowed up by tubes and machines. She had a strange collar around her neck and needles pushing human medicine into her veins. Her arm was completely encased in a large, hard shell that had been wrapped to keep her broken bones from moving. Her leg as well, but the skin I could see was a terrifying shade of purple and black, and swelling. She was severely injured. As I looked at her, I could hear the green Riven's taunting laughter as he'd used his magic to breathe her scent toward me, to let me know he'd hurt her.

I'd smelled her blood and panicked. Throwing up a hasty

barrier that should keep the humans away for the precious minutes I needed to heal her, I stepped closer to her small body.

Fury pumped through me and the glow of my eyes lit her white bedding and her pale face with a faint yellow shine.

With effort, I held myself in check, pulled the magic back until the glaring fluorescent lighting took over once more. She didn't need me to kill anything at the moment, she needed me calm enough to heal her. And I would, if it killed me to do it.

Nothing mattered more than saving her. Nothing. Without her, I was as good as dead. I'd been hanging on by force of will alone for too long. The splinter in my mind was growing, the pain, at times, almost unbearable. But I fought the urge to surrender, to allow the magic to splinter my mind and make me what I hunted. I had hung on for Zach before. And for the hope of finding her.

Brittany.

Calling to the very depths of my soul for the magic, I stepped forward and placed one hand on her injured leg, on the flesh, and the other on the side of her face.

I'm here, love. You're going to be all right. I promise.

She didn't respond, which wasn't a surprise. We weren't fully bonded, and until she accepted me into her heart and mind, I wouldn't be able to communicate with her as I did with my rider. I knew, logically, that kind of bond would take time. Especially as Brittany had no idea what kind of creature I was.

She still thought I was human. Zach's twin brother. A one-night stand. A fling that Zach and I could walk away from. The truth was that I was dragon, and I had made my choice. She was mine. There was no arguing or pleading with the primordial dragon that dwelled within me. I was not human. I had enough honor to let her go, should that be her choice. But without her, I would splinter, kill my rider, be hunted by the others. Zach and I would be no more if this beautiful creature wasn't strong enough to love us. To accept the truth.

We let her believe because she needed to feel safe and the truth would terrify her. So many lies.

Leaning over, I placed my forehead on her chest and pushed healing dragon fire into her broken body. She was Dragonborn, her cells able to use what I gave her to heal as a primitive human could not. I poured my heart into her. My life. I called upon my connection to Zach, and to my mother, the queen of dragons. I needed magic, and I would steal it if I had to, kill if I had to, to keep her alive.

I pushed deeply into my mate's body, searching for her life force, her soul. I needed her to fight, to help me heal her. I found the light of her life, her energy, swirling around her heart and I pushed heat and love to her, merging my light with hers, surrounding her with comfort and love. Letting her know I was there, keeping her safe.

When the magic died and her body refused to accept more, I pulled my energy back and lay unmoving, spent. Near death. My magic depleted beyond anything I'd ever done before. My mother, the queen, would feel me here, on the brink. She would know something terrible had happened to one of her own.

Pressing my ear to Brittany's heart, I let the now steady beat soothe me. She was stronger, out of danger, her body healed. The doctors would scramble for explanations, but I could not allow my mate to suffer just to avoid rousing humans' suspicions.

I sacrificed much to protect all humanity. This once, I would choose to protect what was mine first. My heart. My soul. My mate.

Brittany.

She gasped, as if she'd heard me, and her free hand rose to tangle in my hair. She ran her fingers through the strands, her fingertips caressing my scalp so that I nearly succumbed to sleep.

"Iavo? Are you all right? Where's Zach?" Brittany asked. "Are you going to tell me what's going on? Am I in a hospital?"

She asked about me first? About Zach? She was the one lying on the brink of death in a hospital bed. She was the one who had survived an attack by the Riven. An attack that was my fault. I braced for her anger, for the hurt I knew would be in her voice when she learned the truth. *You have every right to be angry. We never meant for you to get involved in any of this. We came to hunt the beast that attacked you today.*

She froze and her heart raced. "Why can I hear you inside my head?"

I knew, when my soul wrapped around hers, I knew I had taken away her choice, but I couldn't take it back. Didn't want to. *I imprinted on you. We are mated. Now you can hear me as Zach does.*

"Imprinted? What's that supposed to mean? You're not a baby bird."

No. I am a dragon.

"Oh God. I thought I was hallucinating. He was green. A dragon. He threw me in the air and tossed me around like a rag doll. He breathed ice! I thought I was tripping. But I wasn't, was I?

No. We were sent here to hunt him, to bring him to justice. I failed my queen. I failed you. Please forgive me. I lay unmoving, praying she could still love me after I had failed her, allowed her to be hurt. It was a mistake I would not make again. I would hunt the Riven without mercy, without sleep.

As soon as I knew Brittany would be all right.

Her hand moved to the back of my neck, soothing me with a touch in a way no one had ever been able to do before.

"There is nothing to forgive, Iavo. You saved me."

I sat up and shook my head, tucked a strand of hair behind her ear. As I inspected her for further injury, I noticed there were still splatters of blood on her perfect face. I got up and grabbed a wet-wipe and softly rubbed the dried blood from her soft skin.

Her hand gently came up to cover mine, her eyes gazing up, looking for answers I wasn't sure I could give her. "Please," she said, her voice barely a whisper. "Tell me what's happening. Where is Zach? What is going on? Why did that monster attack me?"

I nodded and lowered my hand. But I needed to touch her, to soothe the hurt I saw in her eyes. Leaning forward, I held her gaze and gently pressed my forehead to hers. *Because you are mine. He must have scented me on your skin. I am sorry, mate. I should not have touched you before he was dead, but I could not wait. I needed you. I was too close to splintering.*

When I mentioned scenting, she rubbed her hand in an odd fashion on the bedding, as if remembering something that made her uneasy. "Splintering into what?"

A Riven. A dragon who has lost his soul to evil. A merciless killer. Without you, my mind would splinter and I would become what he is.

"And what about Zach? Is he…like you?"

No. He is like you. Dragonborn. The blood of the dragons runs through his veins, but he is human. He is my rider.

"So, he's not your brother?"

We are closer than brothers. We are dragon and rider. Bonded at my birth. One cannot survive without the other.

"And the twin thing? What's with that?"

I grinned and kissed her gently on the lips. I couldn't help it. From death's door to twenty questions without screaming. That was my courageous mate. *My magic allows me to take a human form. When we are young, newly hatched, our rider is most familiar to us and so we take the form of our rider. The twin explanation makes it easier for humans to accept us when we are together. It allows him to speak for me.*

"Like in the bar, when we first met."

Yes. I knew you were ours, but I needed his help to get you to the cabin.

She leaned back on the pillow and closed her eyes, as if remembering our night together. "Yes, well, you did just fine on your own after that."

I tossed the wet-wipe aside and came to sit down again, but the move was more from necessity than choice. I reached for Zach.

Zach, I am about to collapse. Get me out of here.

Forgetting that Brittany could hear me now, I was shocked when her hand came to my shoulder to steady me. "What's wrong? Tell me what to do."

It is nothing, love. I used all of my magic healing you.

Her eyes widened as she looked at me with obvious shock. "What does that mean? Are you going to be okay?"

I nodded and hoped like hell I wasn't lying as I collapsed in the bed next to her. *You're mine, Brittany. No one will ever hurt you again.*

The protective ward I'd been holding to keep the humans away as I healed my mate faltered when I did and a nurse walked into the room. The young man I'd seen with Zach earlier. My clothing was different from what Zach wore, but the nurse's gaze didn't get past my face and he assumed I was my rider.

"You were supposed to be in the waiting room, sir. You can't be back here. We have to take your wife to radiology."

Brittany sat straight up in bed and the nurse looked at her with big eyes and a slack jaw.

"I think he's in shock. He fainted or something. Can you help him lie down somewhere?"

rittany

THEY ESCORTED Iavo out of the room, the nurse looking confused. But Iavo, the man I loved—no the *dragon* I loved—grinned at me as he allowed the nurse to lead him back to the waiting room.

The second he was gone, Zach slipped inside. "How are you feeling?"

"Me?" I waved the heavy splint around, irritated that I still had the dead weight on my arm, and started unwinding the stretchy bandage that held it in place. "I'm feeling much better," I said, smiling a bit. "But I'm worried about Iavo. And you look like hell."

He did. His skin was pale. His normally bright green eyes glazed over with exhaustion or pain, I couldn't tell which.

Zach came over to me and leaned down for a kiss. "You had us very worried, you know."

I nodded and blinked to hold back tears. My men were here, looking after me, caring about me. I hadn't had that in a long, long time. I wrapped my good arm around him and clung. "I'm so sorry."

"Shh," Zach said. "No apologizing. This wasn't your fault. It was ours."

I shook my head as Zach wiped away a tear. "That's what Iavo said, but I don't—"

"You spoke with Iavo?" he asked. "You can hear him?"

The corner of my mouth turned up again. "Yes. In my mind. Guess it's dragon telepathy. Or magic. I don't know. All I know is that after he healed me, I could hear him."

Zach's gaze held mine, the intensity there almost frightening. "And you aren't upset?"

I kissed him. Hard. "He said you were mine, Zach. That both of you are mine. Is that true?"

"Yes."

I kissed him again. "Forever?"

"If you'll forgive us. We should have been there. Should have protected you." He leaned in and pressed his forehead to mine, just as Iavo had done. But this was Zach, and where Iavo was power and dominance, Zach was gentle and made me feel safe.

"There's nothing to forgive."

His eyes closed, as if my words hurt him. "We will kill the one who hurt you, love. I swear it. No one will ever hurt you again."

"What the hell is going on here?" The voice barked at Zach like a drill sergeant, but my man didn't even flinch.

"I am caring for my wife."

"I just took you to the waiting room. *Again.*" I peeked around Zach's shoulder to see a very frazzled young man in nurse's scrubs glaring at both of us. "How did you get back in here?" The nurse's gaze dropped to Zach's shirt, and the confusion in his eyes intensified. "And weren't you wearing a t-shirt a minute ago? Dark blue?"

Zach's gaze met mine and I burst into laughter. "You better go," I whispered.

Zach kissed me gently on the lips. "Iavo will be able to hear you now, if you need him. We will be close."

"Okay." I nodded and kissed him one more time before he got up and walked past the stunned nurse with a grin on his face nearly identical to Iavo's.

No wonder the poor man was so confused.

Stifling a smile, I finished unwrapping the bandage around the splint and the thing fell to the floor with a loud thud.

The nurse swung back around. "No! You shouldn't—"

He stopped mid-sentence as I flexed and straightened my arm, testing it out.

No pain. Nothing. Even the skin was perfect.

I was so going to make this up to Iavo. Maybe with my mouth around his cock. Or giving him total access to my body for hours. Days. Whatever he wanted. I was getting wet and achy just thinking about it.

"Doctor Wethers? I think you need to come back in here." The nurse turned and left as I reached up to take the annoying neck stabilizer off. I felt like my neck was on stilts.

I had the thing in my lap and was working on my thigh when the doctor, whose voice I recognized as the kind man who'd helped me when I first arrived, walked into the room with the nurse right behind him.

"Brittany? What is going on here? What are doing? Radiology is on the way. You shouldn't be moving."

I smiled. "I'm fine, Doctor. Really. I think I was just in shock and overreacting to everything. Everything hurt when I came in, but I think it was more mental than anything. You know?" Lifting my healed leg, I pulled the hard board-like splint from beneath it and held it out for the nurse.

He looked at the doctor who stepped forward, took the splint, handed it off to the nurse, and proceeded to examine me all over again.

"I don't understand." He turned to the nurse. "Do we have any x-rays we can look at? Anything?"

The nurse looked down at the computer tablet in his hand. "No. Just the lab, and that was mostly normal."

I didn't want more needles. More tests. I wanted to go home and be with my men, make sure Iavo was all right. "I'd like to go now. Can you get this IV out of me?" I held my good arm out to the nurse. He looked to the doctor for permission. The doctor nodded with a shrug.

"All right. I can't explain what just happened, but I did a full examination and you appear to be perfectly healthy."

I winced as the plastic thing came out of my vein and the nurse put cotton over it for me to hold in place as he grabbed the tape. "So, I can go?"

"I'll have then get the discharge paperwork started."

"Thanks, Doctor. I really just want to go home and sleep."

He raised a brow and I could see a dozen questions in his

intelligent gaze, so I pasted on my *dumb-blonde* smile and blinked like there wasn't a thought in my silly, little head.

He wasn't buying it, but he did leave me alone. As soon as the nurse was done with IV torture, I looked around. "Where are my clothes?"

The nurse brought them to me and placed them in my lap. They'd been cut off my body. But in addition to that, they were ripped and torn, covered in blood. God, how the hell had I survived *that?*

I must have paled because the nurse put his hand on my back and leaned in to make sure I didn't topple over. "You sure you feel all right? We can run more tests."

"I'm fine." I was, but there was no way in hell I was going home in *these.* "Are there some surgical scrubs or something I can borrow to wear home? I really don't want to put those back on."

He smiled. He was young, handsome, and had kind eyes. But he watched me like he expected answers, and I wasn't about to give them to him. "Can you tell me what really happened here?"

"Just a mix-up. I must have panicked. I'm sorry to be a bother."

"Panic, huh?"

When I remained silent, he sighed.

"I'm not supposed to do this, but I don't blame you. I'd burn them, if I were you. You should be dead right now."

And *that* was the understatement of the year.

WE WERE BACK at the cabin. We'd called a taxi at the hospital and it took me and Zach working together to get Iavo into bed. Turned out a dragon was damn heavy in his human form.

That was twenty-four hours ago and he hadn't moved.

Zach and I were both showered, rested, well fed...and worried.

"How long is he going to be like this?" I asked. I was lying next to Iavo in bed, my leg thrown over his, my arm around his waist. I wanted him to know I was there.

"I don't know. He's never been this close to the edge before."

"The edge?" I'd heard the odd note in Zach's voice. The worry. "What edge? Dying? You mean he could die because he healed me?" That was not acceptable. No.

Rather than lie to me, Zach turned away, which made me want to scream at both of them.

"Why? Why would he do that?" I buried my face in his shoulder, trying to get closer. "That's stupid. You don't even know me."

"You are our mate, Brittany. Without you, we would not survive. You are our life now. Our beating heart. We are yours."

I shook my head and glared at him. "I don't understand. We just met. This is stupid."

It is our way, mate. You were mine the moment I saw you.

"Iavo!" I leapt up so that I was on my knees, looking down at him. "You're awake? Can you hear me? Talk to me."

Zach came to sit on his other side on the bed and my mate, my *dragon*, opened his golden eyes to stare at me. They were glowing, like they were on fire from the inside. Zach grinned. "The queen decide to take mercy on you?"

Finally. Yes. She does not appreciate when her sons borrow power without permission.

"Borrow power? Like magic?"

The queen helped heal you, Brittany. I could not have done it alone. Your wounds were extensive and I was weak from our battle.

"You could have died, you stubborn fool." Zach's voice was gruff and I understood the sentiment very well.

"Don't do that again, Iavo. I mean it. Let the doctors take care of me next time. I would have been just fine."

There will be no next time, *mate. The Riven dies today.* His voice was fierce. Protective. And I loved him all the more for it.

Leaning over, I kissed him. Hard. Deep. With all the longing I felt. I needed them to make me forget the last two days of hell. Of pain. Of worry. I needed to feel alive.

When Iavo was panting for breath, his hand on my hip, exploring the curve of my ass, I lifted my head and reached for Zach, pulling him toward me so I could kiss him as well. They were both mine. I understood that now in a way I hadn't before. Two halves of a whole. That's how I'd begun thinking of them, and now I knew it to be true.

"Hmm…" Zach moaned, his deep voice reverberating in my ears. His eyes narrowed again. "Be careful. You're still very weak."

Smiling, I stood next to the bed and quickly stripped naked. "I'll show you weak, dragon rider."

Before I could even process what was happening, Zach was on top of me on the bed, his legs on either side of my waist as he straddled me. He was bent at the waist, his hands now wrapped around my wrists. He leaned down and brushed his lips against mine before pulling away without a kiss.

"Oh, no," Zach said. "I don't think so. Not yet."

He leaned forward and then lightly kissed my cheeks, and

then my forehead. With Zach occupying my attention span, I hadn't had time to wonder what had happened to Iavo. I gasped when Iavo's hands wrapped around my ankles as he pulled my legs apart.

Zach raised my hands up over my head and lowered his lips so they brushed over mine. "I want you to stay right there, just like this. You're not allowed to move your hands from that spot. Do you understand?"

I nodded. "Yes."

Zach moved to sit at the foot of the bed next to Iavo. I watched as Zach took hold of my other leg, massaging it. They both stared into my eyes and studied me as they slowly moved their way up my legs. When they reached my thighs, they leaned over and began placing kisses on them. With as synchronized as their mouths were, I knew they were communicating with telepathy. It was cheating, but I loved it. That was the kind of teamwork I could get used to.

The guys moved my legs up and out so they bent at the knees, spreading me open wider, my wet core on display. They took turns, placing open-mouthed kisses on my knees before slowly licking me all the way to the top, carefully missing what I needed most and stopping in the sensitive juncture between hip and thigh. I was caught between painful need and glorious pleasure.

I fought the urge to beg them for what I really wanted with every teasing kiss. I forced my hands to still by my head as I watched them move across my stomach and up to my breasts. I felt like screaming, but didn't want to risk them stopping.

Instead, I did my best to relax, watching their every move,

biting my lip when the urge to beg became too much. My body flushed as my temperature rose with every lick, every kiss.

Zach pulled my right nipple into his mouth, earning a loud moan from me while Iavo positioned himself between my legs. Zach nibbled and played with it while my mind raced, thinking of what was about to happen.

"Please!" I said. The word bubbled out. I couldn't hold it in any longer.

"Please what, gorgeous?" Zach asked.

"Please don't stop. I need you. Both of you. Please... Just—don't stop."

At that moment, Iavo shoved my legs apart once again before leaning in and taking a long, slow lick of me. I nearly growled, my head falling back as I lifted my hips to meet his gifted mouth while Zach continued massaging and tasting my breasts.

"Is that what you wanted?" Zach asked.

"Yes!" I cried out.

Iavo pulled away long enough to slide a finger deep inside of me, earning another growl from me, his toy.

"Please, let me use my hands," I pleaded. "I want to touch you."

Zach smiled and pulled off his shirt. My hand was immediately on his hot skin, touching every curve of his hard chest and tight stomach. I focused on the way Iavo's tongue felt with its every flick against me. Iavo slid a second finger inside me, stretching me open, fucking me slowly as he sucked and flicked at the sensitive nub. *You're mine. This pussy is mine.*

"Yes." There was no denying it, not with both of them

surrounding me, touching me, making me forget anything else existed.

The pleasure was too much. I tugged at Zach's pants, trying to get them undone. He laughed at my enthusiasm and helped me.

In moments, his cock was freed from his jeans and in my hand. Iavo's fingers pressed hard against my g-spot as his lips encircled my clit and he sucked me into his mouth, flicking his tongue over my clit like it was ice cream.

My hand tightened into a hard fist around Zach's length and my breath caught in my throat.

I cried out as Iavo played me like an instrument and my body arched off the bed as my orgasm rushed through me. Zach moved closer and my mouth closed over him, a growl of his own escaping his throat.

My pussy still in spasm, Iavo lifted my hips from the bed and filled me with his cock in one hard, deep stroke. I whimpered with need as he worked his huge cock in and out, pounding into my body, prolonging my orgasm until it seemed to go on and on.

The vibrations coming from my throat, the hard suction I had on Zach's cock made him arch his back and press deeper, hitting the back of my throat as I swallowed him down, rubbed the sensitive bundle of nerves under his length as hard and fast as I could. His pleasure-induced sounds only pushed me on, driving me wild. I tightened my lips around him and moved my tongue against his solid shaft as I sucked.

The wilder Iavo became, the more I lost my mind, my focus, pouring my energy into making Zach as mindless with pleasure as I.

Unable to maintain his position, he collapsed over me on all fours while I moaned both from the need to taste more of him and from Iavo's skill. Though Zach's arms were shaking, he put all of his weight on one while the other hand moved to massage my breasts. He plucked and rolled my nipples, timing the movements to Iavo's thrusting.

Zach pulled away from me with a shout, taking his cock from my mouth as I gasped. Iavo thrust deep. Hard.

His cock pulsed inside me like a wild thing and my pussy walls were so swollen and achy I could feel the slightest shift, the bucking of his shaft as he filled me with heat. His eyes glowed so brightly the room was lit with a golden glow.

"You're so beautiful." The words burst out of me, but Zach groaned and dropped down for a kiss, claiming my mouth with his, exploring me with his tongue. Branding me as Iavo filled me with a fire that had my back arching off the bed.

My orgasm started in my toes, building, filling me up until I screamed as Iavo pumped in and out of my pussy, his cries mingled with mine.

I couldn't move. Couldn't breathe. I was surrounded my men and heat and pleasure.

Zach had barely taken his mouth away when I was flipped over onto my stomach and pulled up on all fours. Iavo moved to the head of the bed and laid on his side, lounging like a lazy cat. He looked well pleased. Very satisfied.

Happy.

I crawled forward so I could kiss him. I wanted his mouth. But as I moved to touch him, Iavo buried his fingers in my hair and held me still, so close the heat of his breath fanned my lips. He held me, his grip unforgiving, and his silent command to hold still, to wait, was so hot I had to close my eyes to hold back a cry of pleasure. My eyes popped open as Zach entered me from behind, slowly. His hands were on my ass, pulling my pussy open for his invading cock, holding me open for his pleasure.

They had gotten very good at keeping me distracted enough to surprise me—and it only added to the intensity. I cried out as he pulled back and filled me with a fast, unexpected thrust.

It took a lot of work to steady myself on my arms while Zach filled me from behind, his hips slamming hard into me with every thrust. His large size coupled with the strength he used to fuck me, I knew that it wouldn't take long to send me over again.

I pulled against the fingers tangled in my hair. I wanted Iavo's mouth. Hungered to taste his chest. The heated skin of his neck. His mouth.

My dragon shook his head and held my gaze. *I want to watch you fuck him.*

Iavo watched. He noticed the way my breasts swayed beneath me as Zach's hard thrusts rocked me forward. He watched my eyes glaze with lust when Zach lifted his hands to my shoulders and used them for momentum to fuck me even harder. I would have fallen forward, my body suddenly weak from how good he felt, but Iavo held me up, one hand in my hair, the other on my chest to steady me.

Iavo wrapped his fingers in my hair and pulled me up far enough that he could kiss me. Finally. I moaned into his mouth as Zach fucked me relentlessly, his heavy breathing matching mine. My entire body began to shudder as another orgasm began to take me.

Come for him. Iavo ordered. *Come now, but look at me. I want to see your eyes when you come all over his cock.*

I could only respond with a nod as I felt my release building to something so monstrous I was afraid I'd lost control of my body. Collapse. Scream. Faint.

"Oh my god."

Iavo held my stare as Zach shocked me. One hand disappeared from my shoulder and landed with a sharp slap on my clit.

I screamed, my body lost. I didn't exist anymore, not alone. They were part of me and I was part of them. Mine.

I didn't fight the spasms that shook me, or the intense aftershocks that I felt with every fast thrust of Zach's bucking cock as he filled me with his seed.

The slight sting of Iavo's hand in my hair held me steady, kept me from disappearing into a million shiny stars in the cosmos. Without him, I would have disappeared.

When it was over, Iavo finally released me, pulling me forward so that Zach's cock slipped free of my wet heat and my head rested on his chest. His heart beat at an odd pace, too slow and too loud to be human.

When he shifted onto his side and Zach slid into place behind me, I knew I was in love. I had no idea what was going to happen to the three of us, but at the moment, I didn't care.

Sleep, love. I will keep you safe.

Iavo's deep voice slipped inside my head as if he'd been speaking to me this way my entire life. It was intimate, and odd, and I loved the way he felt inside me. Like he belonged.

Zach shifted behind me, his arm wrapping around my waist from behind to cup my breast. He was mine, too, and his touch felt as perfect as Iavo's words had. "Sleep, mate, Iavo will take first watch." He lifted his head for a second to look at his dragon. "Wake me up in four hours."

Sleep.

I laughed. "He's going to ignore you, Zach."

Zach chuckled and kissed me on the back of the neck. "What else is new?"

I fell asleep with a smile on my face.

rittany

STRETCHING WAS RATHER difficult with two men wrapped around me. After some impressive, almost acrobatic movements, I managed to shimmy out from under Iavo's arm and crawl out from under Zach's leg.

The men didn't stir, and I took the opportunity to go get cleaned up. I looked at them in complete awe of their beauty and then flushed. I might have to make it a cold shower if I ever wanted to get to my brother.

Once I had dried off, I was sad I only had the borrowed hospital scrubs from the night before to put on. A fresh shirt would be nice. Maybe I would buy a shirt from the book store at my brother's school, I thought. Show some school spirit or something.

I pulled my shirt on before going back out and was met by two naked and beautiful men sitting on the edge of the bed with their arms crossed.

"We would have showered with you," Zach said as he smirked at me.

Iavo nodded in the kind of unsettling, emotionless way he had. He was back to hunting mode and the change in him would have terrified me if I'd been his prey.

"I would have enjoyed that," I said, "but I have to be going, and I have a feeling that would have turned into a long shower."

Zach stood and walked into the bathroom. I watched him walk by with admiration. He was one *damn* good-looking man. Iavo came over and pulled me into his chest. He brought his mouth down hard on mine and kissed me like he was making a mark. When he pulled away, I was breathless, and my knees were a bit weak. The pull between us was impossible to deny. I wanted them every moment of every day.

He made a move to pull me towards the bed, but I resisted— hard as it was. If I lay back down with either of them, I'd never make it to see Garrett. That was the whole reason for being in the city, and I wasn't going to veer from my path. "Not right now, Iavo. You have to hunt a rogue dragon, and I have to go find my brother."

No. It's too dangerous.

I shook his hand off my wrist and stepped back. "Yes. He's my brother and I have to find him."

Zach came out of the bathroom. "Where are you going, love?" he asked with a smile, but there was tension around his eyes and mouth, and I knew he was communicating with Iavo and not including me. No denying, the way he said 'love' made my stomach feel warm, but I wasn't getting detoured. Not today.

"To see my brother. When I went to his dorm, he wasn't there. I'm not about to miss out on the opportunity to talk to him. I've looked for him for too long."

The brothers looked at one another for a moment before turning their gaze back on me.

It's too dangerous. We will take you to see your brother once the Riven is dead and no longer a threat to you.

Iavo was being demanding and dominant, but I wasn't in the mood. Not today. Not about this. I could have died yesterday, and he never would have known I was looking for him. That I'd worried about him every single day we'd been apart. That I loved him. "No. I'm not going to run around afraid of a stupid dragon."

"Brittany, baby, I don't think—" Zach was using a tone of voice I'd heard before. Coaxing. Sweet. But in the end, he wanted the same thing Iavo did. Which was for me to sit here with a target on my back and hope the nasty green monster didn't find me again.

"How do you know I'd be safe here?" I demanded. "He found me at work. He knows my scent. Are you telling me he couldn't find this cabin? Track your dragon scent to this place? If he's not stupid, he'll know you have me here. The moment you leave, I'm a sitting duck."

Zach looked to Iavo.

We will take her to Washington and leave her with the queen. Once she is safe, we will continue the hunt.

"Washington? I thought you were from Arizona?" It surprised me their queen was so far away. I had remembered them mentioning going with them before, but I didn't think it was a hard request. I thought it might have been for a trip, or maybe even just as a suggestion. I had just assumed they were from Chicago. There were millions of people in this stupid city. What was two more?

"Yes, you're our mate. You can't deny the bond; I know you feel it." Zach nodded his head, taking a step closer. "We can leave you under the queen's protection and resume the hunt once you are taken care of."

My anxiety returned then as I realized what was happening. I was being asked to make a choice between them and my brother, or so that was the way it seemed to me. That wasn't an option. Not after all I had gone through to find Garrett and get to him.

I swallowed, trying to calm myself before I spoke. "I just found my brother, and you want me to leave him now? With a deranged dragon serial killer on the loose in his city? No. No freaking way. I am *not* going anywhere."

Without hesitation, without a moment of consideration or empathy, Iavo said, *Yes, you are.* Iavo wasn't wavering. *Our queen resides under the mountain in Washington. She will keep you safe while we finish the hunt. Once we are sure things are safe, we will come for you and take you to our home.* It didn't seem like he'd compromise at all, and that just made me angrier.

"In Arizona?"

Yes. That is our territory. We do not normally travel this far north but followed the Riven here.

I took a deep breath and sighed heavily, my fists clenched at my sides as I tried to get control of myself. I felt completely disrespected, and I wasn't happy about it. "Look… I'm going to see Garrett and then we can discuss *potentially* going to Washington, or Arizona, or wherever you guys are from. I'm not your toy, and we've not known each other long enough for you to simply *tell* me I have to do something. Correction, *no* man can tell me I *have* to do something. Ever. And if that's what you need in a woman, you've got the wrong damn one."

My attempt at control had all been lost the moment I'd opened my mouth. My voice was getting rougher. The problem I was facing was I was in love with them. The truth was that going to Arizona to start a new life with them sounded great. I had always wanted to pack up and travel, move somewhere new and start a new life.

But that wasn't possible.

Not now.

No matter how I felt about them, things weren't just black and white. There was a grey area—one they would have to understand. My brother was the thing that threw a wrench in that plan, and I would absolutely have to choose family, even though he was a stranger to me now. Just because we didn't know each other well now didn't mean that it always had to be that way. We could become close, and I wanted that chance. I wouldn't allow the guys to take that away from me.

And if they cared about me, about what I wanted or needed, they wouldn't ask it of me.

Iavo looked as tense as Zach sounded. He was pacing in front of the bed staring at me. Both of them seemed upset and confused that I would consider anything other than what they had told me.

I shook my head. "I'm going to see Garrett and you're going to go hunt a crazy dragon. *That* is what's happening today." I knew they couldn't force me to go with them. It just felt like it would have been a lot more romantic if they had asked.

Breaking me from my raging thoughts, Iavo pulled me to him and kissed me. His kiss was urgent, forceful, and made my knees melt.

"Don't worry. I'll be fine. I'll be safer in the city than I will be out here alone."

Iavo let me go, his eyes glowing with the amber light I now realized only came with high emotion.

Zach stepped forward and placed his lips against mine. His kiss was a lot softer than Iavo's had been. "Be safe. Stay out of sight if you can. If you go out, stay under cover. Be careful."

"I will. I promise."

"We'll find the Riven and come for you."

"Okay." I was worried the Riven would hurt them. Kill one of them. But I didn't want to put the thought into their minds. Confidence was key when heading into battle, and I didn't want to be the weakling in our relationship. Still, I couldn't hold back the words, "Come back to me."

He will die a painful death, mate. I give you my word.

I wasn't sure if that was supposed to be romantic, coming from a dragon, so I didn't say anything as I made my way out the door.

rittany

THE SKY HAD TURNED into streaks of gold as I wiped the tears from my eyes. I dropped the sun visor to protect my vision from the worst of it while driving. I'd had to call a taxi to take me back to my car, but I felt a bit better the moment I was back inside my own property.

The car wasn't anything fancy, but it got me wherever I needed to go. There was this deep ache inside me the farther I got from the guys. I wondered if it was the bond they spoke of pressing on me or if it was my own emotions.

Maybe I shouldn't have left without them, but I certainly couldn't live without my brother, and they were dead set on the hunt for this Riven. Garrett and I were separated as children when we went into the system. I swore to him once I found him, I'd never let him go again.

The skyline of Chicago came into my view as I took the exit to the university. Dread welled up in me as I tried to calm my nerves. As if seeing my brother was a huge event. The university came into sight as I pulled into the parking spot closest to his dorm.

I rushed out into the humidity, opened the door, and looked down the hallway. I could see his door on the right. I made a beeline to it. This time, I didn't feel like fucking with any stupid roommate. Without hesitation, I opened the door, startling my brother and his roomy in the process. There he was… I couldn't believe it. With just as much gusto, I ran forward. He started to laugh as I wrapped my arms around him.

"Where the hell have you been? I've been looking for you forever!" Garrett asked with obvious anger.

I just shook my head, and let the tears fall, unsure of how to answer. Every time we were separated I felt like I was falling apart. Maybe Garrett did also.

Shaking my head and stepping away, I said, "It's okay, I'm here now. I met someone. That's where I've been. You disappeared and scared the shit out of me." I patted him on the back and pulled back.

Tears started to flow from my eyes again as I sat down at his desk. When I looked up at him, his dark eyes betrayed him as well, tears streaming down his own cheeks.

"Well, since you're here, why don't we go out and get a drink or two?" Garrett asked as he stood up and pulled me from my seat.

I laughed and let him lead the way. He led me to the parking lot and out to his Jeep. Once we were all settled in, we went. It only took a few blocks to get to the bar, but we chatted the whole way.

The bar was surprisingly not as busy as I had expected. We took two stools at the bar top, instead of opting for one of the tables, and I ordered a nice, neat tumbler of apple whiskey. Garrett ordered a dark ale and we sat and enjoyed each other's company. The other patrons started to get loud and a few fists were thrown, so we moved away from the melee to a booth in the corner and hoped it didn't spill over into our area.

My brother seemed happy, and I couldn't help but be happy for him. "I only have a semester left until I graduate! I took the LSAT. Now I wait."

"Wait for what?"

"Answers from the schools I applied to." He grinned at me like I was confused, which I was.

"But, you're graduating. I'm confused."

He laughed, a real laugh, the first time I'd heard that sound from him and something broken inside me healed in an instant. He was okay, my baby brother. Really okay.

"Law school."

I nearly choked on my drink. "What?"

"If Mom and Dad could see us now, what do you think they'd say?" Garrett asked as he sipped his drink.

Still reeling with the idea of my baby brother going to law school, I didn't think to lie, or be diplomatic. "I honestly don't know what they would say. They didn't care about us when we were little, so I don't think they'd care about what we have going on now. I just want to enjoy the fact that you're rocking school, and you're about to have one hell of a life," I said as I picked up my whiskey and sipped. I motioned to the waitress for another, and with a quick nod, she acknowledged me.

Garrett sat back and drank the remainder in his glass. The waitress dropped off my new drink on the way to the kitchen. "Who are you seeing now?" Garrett asked.

"We'll talk about that later; it's a little complicated. How about you? I heard there was a girl you're seeing. Who's she?" I smiled as I asked.

Garrett blushed slightly and answered, "Well, there is a woman I'm seeing named Megan. She's amazing. I'm thinking about proposing, but I'm not sure yet. And besides, if I decide to go for it, I want to wait until graduation night to ask her."

My eyes widened as the biggest smile spread across my face. "Oh, my god! That's amazing news!" I screamed and jumped from my seat to hug him. I drew the attention of the entire bar, but I didn't care. I was going to hug my brother whether the whole fucking bar agreed with it or not.

"Let's get a couple of shots to celebrate! Mary! Two more shots of whiskey over here please! We're celebrating!" I said with a laugh as I wrapped Garrett's head in my arm and rubbed my knuckles across his head.

He pulled away but laughed as I took my seat across from him. "Don't go crazy, sis. I said I'm *thinking* about asking her."

It wasn't long before Mary dropped off our shots as she walked by, smiling and giving her congratulations as she did. After all those shots, time with my brother, and a couple tumblers of whiskey, I forgot why I was even sad in the first place.

I paid the bill and we made our way out the door. Next door there was a perfectly placed restaurant, *The Flapjack House*. "My treat, we're going out to have some flapjacks!" I said to Garrett as we drunkenly made our way to the front door.

The only patrons were other like-minded drunks who had obviously been in the same bar as we had. We took a seat in the corner and looked over the menu. I loved just being with my brother. After so many years were stolen from us, I had a lot of time I needed to make up for, and I couldn't wait to get started.

"So, what do you plan on doing when you finish law school?" I asked.

Garrett opened his mouth to speak but was interrupted as the waitress walked up. "What can I get y'all?" The salt-and-pepper-haired woman's nametag identified her as *Marcia*.

My head was fuzzy as I looked at the menu, but I didn't really need to see. I already knew what I wanted. "I'll have three flapjacks, hash browns with onions, and a mocha, but can you add two shots of espresso to that?"

Marcia smiled, nodded then looked to Garrett. "And what can I get for you?"

He paused for a moment as he looked at the menu, but then finally just said, "I'll have the same."

She took our menus and left us. Even though years had separated us from one another, we still had the same taste in food. It was kind of a dumb thing to be excited over, but I would probably be getting excited over a lot of silly things for quite some time to come.

Picking up right where we had left off, he said, "Family law."

Two words and he didn't need to say more. I knew. We both knew why. Lawyers and social workers had separated us. Kept us apart. Given us to other people. Not that staying with our parents had been an option, but that time in our lives had been chaotic and painful. "That's a rough road, little brother."

"I know. But someone has to do it. Who better than me?" The hint of laughter that lingered in his eyes was completely gone now and I knew that look well. Pain. Years of stress and worry. Instability. Never knowing if we were going to spend another night under the same roof or be torn apart. That kind of life left scars where no one could see them. Scars my brother and I shared.

Scars Zach and Iavo were beginning to heal.

Done, we paid and walked arm in arm toward the car. I was blissfully happy, so relieved that Garrett remembered his big sister, that he didn't blame me for the completely messed up version of a childhood we'd both survived.

"I love you, little brother. I never stopped looking for you." I was crying and he turned, pulling me into a hug.

"I know. I love you, too. And now that we're together again, everything will work out. You'll see."

I nodded and wiped at my runny nose as I looked up at him. He was tall, my *baby* brother. Almost as tall as Zach, and built of solid muscle. Whatever girl had her hooks in him was very, very lucky.

My unwavering smile faded as the hair on my body stood straight up. I flinched backward as I saw Garrett get pistol whipped from behind, my brother falling to my feet, unconscious.

Before I could react, the offender lunged at me with the barrel pointed directly at my head. I could feel the cold steel of the gun pressed against my temple. "Leave him alone. He has nothing to do with this."

The golden eyed monster stepped around my brother's body like he was a dead cat on the street. "On the contrary, I smell his blood. He is one of us, Dragonborn. He comes, too. Perhaps I will use him to bargain with the queen."

I almost growled at him. "You'll have me. Why do you need him?"

His laugh made my blood go cold. "You'll be dead. The queen will not bargain for a corpse."

He struck hard and fast. Blinding pain. The sensation of falling.

I landed on top of my brother.

Then…nothing.

I WOKE next to a pile of bodies piled as high as I was tall. There were at least three dozen people—all torn to pieces. I didn't know where one began and another ended. Men, women, probably children… This wasn't like the movies. These creatures didn't care whether it was right or wrong to kill a child. Because the Riven was a true monster. He didn't live by the morals of humans.

Everything around me was overwhelming, especially the horrible stench. I couldn't handle the smell and I turned, vomiting in the dirt to my left. Not wanting to be anywhere near that smell either—thrown-up pancakes and booze—I scooted away from my vomit and the pile of mutilated bodies and saw my brother.

Thank God.

He didn't look good. Too pale. Covered in blood and filth. But he was all in one piece, which gave me hope.

Inch by inch, I clawed my way to Garrett. As I neared him, I looked back, stealing glances as the Riven paced at the opening of the cave entrance. We were in his lair. His den.

Zach and Iavo would come for me…and it appeared the Riven knew it.

When he disappeared on the other side of the cavern, I crawled the rest of the way to Garrett as quickly as I could, not caring that my head spun or that I scraped my forearms raw. He was breathing, but it was shallow, and his head was still oozing blood. Even with all that, it looked as though he had a fighting chance. He probably had a concussion, but a concussion was the least of our worries.

Pulling Garrett's head onto my lap, I held him so he'd know he wasn't alone.

The Riven turned, saw what I had done, and smiled. "Bond with your human. It will cause him more pain when I kill you."

He was an asshole. Certifiable, and a complete asshole. I didn't respond. I wasn't stupid. I knew my mates would come for us. They had to.

Closing my eyes, I called them to mind. Their touch. Their scent. The pleasure I found in their arms. I thought of Zach's gentle kiss and Iavo's rough fingers tangled in my hair. I thought of Iavo collapsing in the hospital room, the grins on both of their faces as they confused the poor nurse, the way they'd always tried to take care of me.

Iavo. Mate. I am here. I need you.

I willed my mind to focus, to call out to the dragon who was our only hope of survival. Tears slipped down my cheeks and fell into Garrett's hair. *I need you, Iavo. I need you so much.*

I am here, love. We are here.

I had to bite my cheek to keep from yelling out in relief, but my captor must have sensed something in the air. His eyes began to glow and he paced like a caged tiger, starved, hurt, and full of rage.

He's crazy, Iavo. Be careful. We are in the back of the cave. By the dead bodies.

The Riven transformed into the beautiful jade dragon he was. He was stunning to look at. It made me sad that something to beautiful could be so evil.

He roared so loudly that I thought he was going to blow my ear drums. I covered my ears the best I could, but it didn't seem to do much good. It echoed off every wall, every stalactite and every stalagmite, damn near piercing through my hearing with every vibration.

I crawled behind the boulder, taking Garrett with me and laying him down so he didn't get hit by any falling debris.

I tucked my legs into my chest and hid my face on my knees. My skin was covered in grey dust.

Drying my tears with my dusty shirt, I pulled Garrett into the nook of my arm. As I did, he moaned in pain and I slapped my hand over his mouth and leaned over to whisper in his ear.

"Shhh, we're not safe here. I need you to be quiet. Just for a little while. Help is coming, but you can't make any noise," I whispered to him as I softly brushed his dusty blond hair out of his face.

My fingers were gentle as I tried to soothe him, careful not to touch the open wound he had from getting pistol whipped in the parking lot. Garrett laid against my bruised arm and I stared off into the darkness of the cavern in a daze.

I wasn't sure if he'd heard me or was unconscious and I prayed that I hadn't found my brother only to lose him. If he died, it was my fault.

I'd led the Riven right to him.

CHAPTER 12

*avo*

THE RIVEN USED Brittany's scent like a lure, laying a trail for me to follow back to his lair. Zach clung to my back with a fury I'd rarely felt from him as I used my large wings to fly faster than I ever had before.

Brittany was hurt. Bleeding. Dying.

I knew the Riven would keep her alive to torment me so he could kill her and make me watch. It was a sick and twisted truth that the Riven loved nothing more than to cause others pain.

Either the dragon wanted to die, or it was a trap. And option number one would make my life too easy.

With dragons, things were *never* that simple.

"How close are we?" Zach yelled the question and I swooped

down out of the clouds almost on top of the dragon's killing den. The stench of dead bodies and dragon so strong I was surprised that Zach couldn't smell it, even with his pathetic human senses.

We are here. I dove down upwind of the dragon's den and tilted my shoulder so Zach would roll onto the ground as I passed by. *Get off. Sneak inside and find her. I'll kill him.*

"Done." Zach rolled, hitting the ground with a grunt as I pumped my wings and rose back up into the air. The moment I sensed Zach was hidden behind the small rise, I bellowed my challenge to the other dragon.

I would strike his heart with my claws, rip his throat from his body, incinerate his wings with my fire. He'd dared touch my mate.

He would die.

～

Zach

HOLY HELL, I'd never seen Iavo like this. Iavo's scream echoed across the water like a cannon, the boom of his power making the surface of the lake ripple as far as I could see.

He was in a killing rage.

When the green dragon roared an answer, I ducked down as low to the ground as possible, fairly certain the Riven would be focused on the golden challenger, but not willing to take any chances. Dragons could smell better than any bloodhound and had better vision than the eagle. They were extremely dangerous, and I was too close to the Riven to do anything stupid.

I didn't dare breathe until the green dragon leapt to the sky with a roar and the two collided in midair.

Horrified and unable to look away, I watched as they ripped at each other with vicious claws, Iavo heaving fire into the other dragon's face with no effect. The green dragon was breathing ice, steam rising and water falling like rain from between them.

Go! Iavo yelled and I bolted from my hiding place to run inside the cave. I found Brittany huddled protectively over her brother. They were both covered in blood, but at least my mate was conscious.

"Brittany, baby, I'm here. We're here."

She started crying but wiped the tears away with a stubborn glare. "Garrett is really hurt. That asshole pistol-whipped him. I think he has a concussion."

I gathered her brother in my arms and waited for her to stand. "Can you walk?"

"Yes. I think so."

"Good. Let's get out of here."

She gagged as we passed the pile of half eaten dead and placed a trembling hand on my shoulder.

"Don't look at them, baby. Just look at me."

"I can't believe this. How do people not know about this?"

We neared the entrance and I peeked outside, checking the positions of both dragons. They were still locked in combat, wings beating frantically as they darted at each other, each going for blood. "What do you think would happen if regular humans knew about dragons?"

Her silence was telling and I knew she wouldn't skirt around the truth. "They'd hunt you down and kill every dragon and rider they could find."

"Yes. All of us. Good or bad."

"Iavo is good. And so are you, Zach."

I carried her brother's unconscious body out onto the shoreline and hoped she was right. About both of us.

Brittany

Knowing something and seeing it are two different things.

I knew dragons were real.

I knew that Iavo was a dragon.

But I fell to my knees on the wet ground as the two dragons, one sparkling emerald green and one shimmering, vibrant amber, locked talons, or claws, or whatever they were called on a dragon—and dove head first into the freezing cold lake.

"Iavo!" I yelled for him as Zach put Garrett down gently and stepped in front of both of us, acting as a shield, watching the fight play out.

"He's okay, but he's going to be angry." Zach looked down at me over his shoulder. "He *hates* cold water."

Zach's laugh distracted me enough that I could ignore the anxiety caused by seeing the large revolver in his hand. The gun was ridiculous, with a barrel that looked at least eight inches long and polished silver. "What are you, the Lone Ranger?"

"Laugh all you want, but this little beauty has saved our lives more than once."

I studied the gun and pulled Garrett's head into my lap. "So what are you waiting for? Shoot him."

"It's a last resort. It won't do much, just piss him off."

The dragons chose that moment to burst from the water and rocket straight up into the air. The green one was bleeding. I could see the dark liquid sliding down his back. One of his wings was torn, almost in two, but it was holding together, and he was going for Iavo's neck with his massive green maw.

I screamed, the vision of Iavo's ripped throat clouding my mind.

Zach stepped forward and raised the gun in one smooth motion, firing as if he'd done it a thousand times.

The green dragon veered off his attack with a scream and turned his eyes on Zach as Iavo recovered.

But it was too late. The Riven changed direction and dove for Zach, a wall of ice pouring out of his giant mouth like white fire.

"Zach!" I screamed even as I rolled away, putting my back to the dragon, trying to shield my brother with my body.

But Zach was running, firing the revolver as he went. The gunfire was loud, almost as loud as the dragons' roars had been, but the green monster kept coming.

And then Zach went down under a wall of ice.

NO! Iavo roared in my mind even as my golden dragon dove hard and fast at the Riven's back.

Lifting my head enough to watch, I saw Iavo land on the other dragon's back, dig his claws into the strong, green neck, and twist.

I winced, turning away as the loud snap and crack of bones filled the air. The green dragon heaved a sigh and flopped to the ground, dead.

Not sure, I looked at my mate. *Iavo, can he heal that?*

No, he cannot.

Iavo landed at once and a swirl of light and color nearly blinded me as he shifted from dragon to human.

Gently, I lay Garrett's head on the ground and rushed to Zach's side. Half of his body was covered in ice, the skin already peeling from some of his flesh, burned from his body as if the ice had, indeed, been flames.

Iavo knelt beside me, and knelt down, placing his forehead to Zach's, his hands on Zach's shoulders. *Hang on, brother. The queen comes.*

"Can't you heal him? Do your dragon thing?" I asked Iavo.

He shook his head. *I am keeping him alive. It is all I can do. This is too much, even for me.*

"But the dragon queen is coming?"

Yes.

"And she can heal him?"

If she finds him worthy.

"What?" What the hell was that supposed to mean? But Iavo was done, moving along the shoreline to check on my brother as I knelt beside Zach. "I love you. Hold on for me, baby," I whispered to him and hoped that somehow he could hear me.

Your brother is stable. Iavo returned and leaned down to gently scoop Zach up into his arms. He led me farther away from the cave entrance and the carnage that was buried within. "What about my brother? We can't leave him out in the open like that."

Come with me. I will come back for him, and I do not wish to leave Zach alone when I do.

"Why don't we just stay here?"

He sniffed, as if the very air was offensive. *My mother would be offended.*

"So? I don't want to leave him."

Come now. We will not go far and I will know if your brother is disturbed.

Well, I didn't want to leave Garrett alone with the pile of dead bodies and a dead dragon just a few steps away, but Iavo didn't leave me much choice, taking off at a steady pace with Zach in his arms. It was either follow, or get left behind. And he was right, I didn't want Zach to be left alone either. At least I knew that everything in the cave was too dead to crawl out and kill my brother. Disgusting and sad, but dead.

Unless zombies were a real thing, too. Which was ridiculous and stupid, but that's what I'd thought about dragons a few days ago. God only knew what other myths or legends were true. Werewolves? Vampires? Aliens? Reptile people? Fairies?

I'd ask my dragon later, when we were alone and there was no one around to laugh at me.

I followed Iavo, who was stark naked and covered with muscle. I'd never been granted an extended view of his backside, but I was so worried about Zach and Garrett that every footstep felt as if I dragged a hundred-pound weight.

When we reached the scruff of woods lining the shore, Iavo carefully placed Zach on the ground and went back to the shoreline for Garrett. I was so grateful for him, for his calm and his strength. He was steady, and he made me steady. Soon, he returned with Garrett and gently laid my brother on the ground next to Zach.

I hunkered down and sat next to Zach and Garrett, taking their hands gently in mine. I used the edge of my shirt to wipe away the blood and dust from Garrett's face. He slowly started to come around as I finished wiping away the evidence of the cave. I really hoped he wouldn't remember anything from that place.

"Shhh, just rest. You're okay," I whispered to Garrett.

Iavo stood up and walked away from us, as if he were headed into the woods. "Iavo? What are you—" The words died in my throat as a stunningly beautiful, voluptuous woman with scarlet red hair, eyes the color of garnets, and skin the color of caramel walked out of the shadows surrounded by two sets of identical twins.

They were all naked. Their bodies? Perfect. Of course.

Good God. More dragons.

The woman was striking, and the only one who was obviously not human. She looked like a fairy queen, an elf, some kind of mythical creature.

Like a *dragon*. She was honestly the most beautiful thing I've ever seen. A walking, breathing goddess. Without introduction, I knew she had to be Iavo's mother, the Dragon Queen.

She turned her eyes on me as she walked up to Zach's prone form on the forest floor. Iavo bent and dropped to one knee before her, a noble son bowing before his queen.

Mother, Zach is mortally wounded. I beg your assistance.

I heard your call, my son. I am here.

Thank you.

I mimicked my mate's words. "Thank you."

She arched a red brow as if my words were an insult.

She placed her hands over Zach's body and the entire area glowed red with her power, the light from her ruby red eyes. She was stunning and frightening to behold.

When Zach's breathing eased, she turned a curious eye to my brother. *Who is the half-dead human? Why is he here?*

She spoke to Iavo, but I answered, prepared to beg. "He's my brother. Please save him."

Again, she ignored me, turning to her son for an answer. Iavo obliged. *He is Dragonborn, Mother. A born rider.*

Very well, my son. But he has seen too much. If he lives, he must choose to live with us.

I was shaking my head before my mind processed her words. "No. He's in school. He wants to be a lawyer. He has a life. A fiancée. He has plans." He was my baby brother and the instinct to shield him flared to life stronger than ever. I didn't care that he was a grown man. He was still mine to protect. And this world, these people, Iavo and Zach were my choice, not his.

The queen turned to glare at me and I wished she hadn't. Her voice was like a thunderclap inside my head. *Not anymore. Now he's mine.*

If she hadn't just saved Zach's life then laid hands on my brother and healed him, I would have punched her in the face.

rittany

THE QUEEN REFUSED to allow Garrett to return to his dorm. I had to watch as one of her naked dragon men turned into a fantastic sky blue and silver dragon. His rider scooped my brother up into his arms, put him up on his dragon's back and took off. I had no idea where they were taking him or what would happen next.

Iavo was watching me with an unreadable expression on his face. Actually, he was watching both of us, me and Zach, as I knelt beside Zach and tried to get him to wake up.

"Why won't he wake up?"

He needs sleep to complete the healing. He will be well by morning. The queen's voice was not so loud this time and I swallowed every last bit of pride and anger I had. She was a dragon, and she'd just saved the lives of two men I loved.

"Thank you."

She nodded her head regally and turned away from me to face Iavo. He immediately dropped to one knee.

Thank you, Mother.

The queen didn't respond but nodded her head slightly before lifting her arms over her head to...transform.

My jaw dropped, I felt it happen, but there was nothing I could do.

Iavo was beautiful in dragon form, shimmering gold and amber, his scales practically glowing whenever the sunlight hit him. But he was different. His dragon jaw made of course angles and sharp teeth. His entire body seemed created for battle, for tearing apart enemies. He was hulking in his size and brute strength. A gorgeous monster, but a monster nonetheless.

This dragon was just as deadly, but everything about her was refined. Beautiful. Ethereal. She was a goddess, a myth come to life. She was a deep, vibrant red, the color of rubies. He scales glowed, but it was as if the light came from within and she needed no external source to make her body shimmer. The red dragon's wings were tucked neatly away, but she was huge, larger than both Iavo and the green dragon he'd fought. And her teeth, although not as big and bulky, looked needle sharp and very deadly.

The other two men she'd brought with her, a matching pair of dragon and rider, dropped to their knees next to Iavo.

If I hadn't already been on my ass on the ground, I think I would have fallen over. The air grew heavy with power and I had to force air into my lungs as she turned her head and stared down at me.

Do you love my son?

Holy shit. Seriously? She was going to ask me that now?

I saw Iavo's body tense out of the corner of my eye, but I didn't dare look away from the queen's gaze, afraid she'd snap that massive jaw down and bite me in half.

But that wasn't why I answered the way I did. Something about her compelled me to tell the truth. "Yes. I love them both."

Take good care of them, Dragonborn, or you will answer to me. Those were the last words she spoke to me before launching straight up into the air. Her guard, or whatever he was, quickly shifted into dragon form, a dark, glistening blue that looked almost black, and his rider leapt onto his back.

To Iavo, she said one final thing. *The hatching ceremony will be in three days. Bring your mate. Our new rider may require her presence.*

Yes, Mother.

Within seconds we were alone and Zach was reaching for me, his shaking hand trying to touch my face. "You love us?"

"Yes, I love you." I wrapped my fingers around his and pulled his palm the rest of the way to rest on my cheek. Tears streaked my face, but I didn't care whether or not he felt them. I was well past the point of hiding anything from these two men —or rather, this man and dragon—that had turned my entire world upside down.

Iavo joined me, kneeling next to both of us. I leaned over and kissed him, gently, on the cheek. "I love you, too, Iavo."

Let's get out of here.

"Please." All I wanted was a hot bath and twelve hours of

sleep with my men curled around me. I never wanted to sleep alone again, afraid visions of dead bodies piled high would haunt my nightmares forever.

But I trusted my mates to keep me safe, to always come for me.

I woke up in the morning alone, my arms reaching out to wrap around my mates and finding nothing but cold sheets and an empty bed.

Unhappy about it, I made my way to the bathroom for my morning ritual, and to brush my teeth. I used extra toothpaste, unable to get the remembered taste of the cave's dirt floor out of my mouth. I knew it was probably all in my head, but the minty burn made me feel better.

I was still naked from my bath last night, and I didn't bother with clothes. My mates liked me naked, and I found I did, too. Especially when they pressed their warm bodies to mine and cradled me as I fell asleep.

Other than the uncertainty over what was going to happen with my brother, I was happier than I'd ever been in my life. And the objects of my affection were nowhere to be found.

Where the hell were they? I discovered I did not like waking up alone.

Done in the bathroom, I opened the door, walked back into the bedroom and padded barefoot back to bed. I had nowhere to go and nowhere to be, and I wanted to be warm, surrounded by their scents. I buried my face in Iavo's pillow just as the door opened.

Zach lifted my hand and kissed the back of it.

"Good morning, love."

The endearment wrapped around me and made me feel even warmer than I already did. I was rested, clean, and my men looked like smoking hot models in their matching black jeans, turtlenecks and leather jackets. It was like I'd woken up in an episode of *The Bachelor*, with *twins*. "Kiss me."

He chuckled and Iavo moved to stand at the end of the bed. He wrapped his hand around my ankle and tugged me toward him. *I am happy to kiss you, mate.*

I raised an eyebrow at Zach as Iavo pulled me to the end of the bed, teasing him with the fact that I was getting my kiss, and he wasn't.

"Iavo, seriously? You know if we start we won't be able to stop."

Iavo ignored him, lifting me into his arms and kissing me like I was the only woman in the world, like I was his air and he'd never get enough of me. It was hot and wet and never-ending, and I melted into him like he was mine.

Because he was. At least my wet pussy thought so. And my aching breasts. And the heart that beat wildly in my chest.

"Iavo. The surprise first." Zach laughed when I moaned in protest but tore my lips free of Iavo's.

"A surprise? You got me something?"

"Yes, love." Zach sat next to me on the bed and Iavo knelt on the floor at my feet. They surrounded me, touching me, and I felt totally loved. Totally safe.

"What is it?" I *loved* surprises, probably because I never got them—unless they were the bad kind, the kind that had me toting my belongings around in a trash bag to the next foster home.

Iavo's eyes were glowing, the amber light making me warm and tingly. *Many things are unsaid between us, mate. But I am yours, heart and soul, we are yours, if you'll have us.*

Zach dropped to his knees next to his dragon and held out a small jewelry box. "We love you, Brittany. We will love you, honor you, cherish you and protect you until our dying breath. Please say yes." He opened the box to reveal a brilliant ruby and diamond ring. The large stone was a deep, rich red that made my heart stutter in my chest.

"Are you asking me to marry you? Both of you? I don't understand."

Zach took the ring out of the box as Iavo placed a kiss on my knee. Then my thigh. *Totally* distracting. "Yes. Dragonborn don't give diamonds, Brittany. Our mates wear rubies to honor the queen, and the sacrifice we all make to protect the planet. Only our mates are allowed to wear red stones. It is a sign of the highest honor and respect among our kind."

"Our kind?" I asked. Iavo lips were nibbling on the side of my hip now, working his way up to my waist, and I was having trouble breathing.

You are Dragonborn, mate. The magic of a dragon sire flows in you veins. You are mine. Iavo punctuated the last by taking my already hard nipple into his mouth and suckling until I moaned, burying the fingers of my right hand in his hair to hold him closer, demand more. My pussy was wet and aching, so empty. I wanted them both. Together.

Mine.

"You're cheating, Iavo." The words were half laugh, half groan as he flicked my nipple with his tongue.

You are mine.

"Ours, dragon. She's ours. And she hasn't said yes, yet." Zach took my left hand and slipped the beautiful ruby onto my ring finger. It fit perfectly. "Please, Brittany. Say yes. Come with us to Arizona, to our home. Live with us. Be mine forever."

Ours.

"Now you want to share?"

You are my rider. She is my mate. You are both mine, Zach. I do not share what is mine.

Iavo moved from one breast to the other and I had to cross my legs, squeeze my thighs to prevent myself from opening them and showing them my wet folds in blatant invitation. They were soooo cheating right now, and I didn't care.

I tilted my head toward Zach and pulled him in for a kiss. I was done messing around. And I knew what I wanted.

Both of them. Inside me. Together. Right now.

"I think I need a sample of what I'll be agreeing to first." Pulling Zach's lips to mine, I smiled as Iavo froze in shock, releasing my nipple from his mouth to look up at me as I kissed Zach.

Being watched was turning me on. And being in control for the first time since I'd met these two powerful, dominant men made me feel edgy and dangerous and very, very sexy. Maybe it was the dragon blood the queen confirmed ran through my veins, maybe it was love, lust, two days of an emotional roller-coaster ride, but whatever it was, I needed them inside me. I needed to know, once and forever, that they were mine.

I knew the bonding of a dragon required Iavo to fill my ass

with dragon magic as Zach filled my pussy. I'd had a taste of it, of both of their attentions, but never together.

Never the way they were born to love me. And I wanted everything.

Turning my head away from Zach, he kissed the side of my neck as I held Iavo's gaze. "I want you both inside me. Now. Right now. I don't want to wait." They both seemed frozen in time until I gave my next request. "Take off your clothes."

They obeyed at once and I leaned back, bracing myself on my hands as I took in the two magnificent men standing before me. A matching pair, their muscled chests led to defined abs and powerful thighs. And between? Two cocks, rock hard and ready for me.

Moving my hand from Iavo's hair to his arm, I traced his muscular shoulder, bicep, forearm, lower until I found his hand and wrapped my fingers around his, pulling toward my center as I opened my legs and settled his hand over the wet welcome there. He shuddered, his eyes glowing brighter as I folded my hand over his and slipped both his finger and my own inside my body. The move was wild and naughty, and the look on his face made me want to do it again and again. So I did, gasping as he pushed his finger deeper, stroking the tip of my womb, pressing my hand against my clit.

Zach's forehead was pressed to my collarbone as he looked down, watching Iavo and I finger fuck me, together. "Brittany." My name was more groan than word and I knew my laughter was pure seductress as I pushed Iavo away, grabbed Zach and rolled him beneath me on the bed. He allowed it, for I never would have been able to force him anywhere he didn't want to be. His knees were at the end of the bed, his feet on the floor, and his cock up and at attention.

I didn't wait, so hot, so ready for him. I climbed over him like a goddess and took his lips as I slid my wet pussy down over his cock, taking him in one long, slow conquest. When he was buried deep, I lifted my lips from his and let him breathe.

"You're mine, Zach."

That moment, fingers wrapped in my hair and tugged me gently until I sat up. I knew who wanted my attention, and I was happy to give it to him.

"Iavo." I sat up, then leaned back, grinding my body down on Zach so that he moaned as I lifted my arms back over my head and searched for my dragon, pulling him down into a kiss. "I want you, too. All three of us. Like it's supposed to be."

He kissed me like I was his air, holding my head still for his conquest as his hot palm slid down my back to cup my ass. Then lower still, to the virgin opening he wanted to claim, and slipped the tip of his finger inside. *I will take you here, mate. Fill your body with my essence, with dragon magic. You will be mine forever. We will be fully bonded. Live together. Die together. Do you understand what you are offering me?*

I kissed him, hard. "Yes. It's called love, Iavo. And I love you both. I want this."

One more hard kiss and he pushed me down, into Zach's waiting embrace. Zach pulled me over into a kiss and I made sure to hold my bottom in the air, where Iavo would have full access, and a clear invitation. I wanted this. I wanted them.

He wasted no time, positioning himself behind me in moments, the warm, hard head of his cock pressing me open slowly.

I'd been expecting cold fingers coated in lubricant, but all I felt was his cock, hard and hot and ready, spreading me open, making me burn.

When the head of his cock popped inside, I gasped and Iavo stopped moving. "Aren't you going to use something? I don't think I can take you like this."

He stroked my back and my ass as Zach chuckled under me, vibrating his hard abs against my clit, making me moan. "Wait for it, mate."

"What—" The words died on my tongue as something happened, something I wasn't prepared for and couldn't explain.

Power. Heat. *Magic* flowed into me and I could feel something warm and wet coating my insides, preparing the way for Iavo's hard cock to fill me.

He pressed forward, an inch. No more. But my entire body shuddered with pleasure, my pussy clamping down on Zach's like a fist. "Iavo."

My dragon leaned over me, pressing kisses to the space between my shoulder blades, the back of my neck, as his essence continued to fill me up, the pleasure building inside me like a tidal wave about to crash onto shore and destroy everything in its wake.

You're mine, Brittany. He pulled out just enough to make me moan, then pressed forward, a bit harder, a little deeper, the warm heat flooding me increased, easing his way, making him slide inside without resistance. *What you feel is a gift of the Dragonborn, your body and mine, connecting. A dragon knows his mate, and my body knows yours, would never hurt you. My magic provides, mate. I am incapable of harming you, would die to protect you. You're mine. I love you, Brittany, and I have never loved another.*

His voice was full of heartache. Years of pain. And a desperate need for acceptance I wasn't sure even he was aware of. "Yes, Iavo. Make me yours."

And then he was inside me, the slight pop of my muscle as it gave way the sign he must have been waiting for as he thrust the rest of the way inside. There was no pain, only heat and fullness and pleasure. Thank God for self-lubricating dragon cocks.

I was so full, stuffed with my men, completely over-whelmed. I started to shake, unable to cope with the pleasure, getting lost in it. It was too much. Too big.

And then they were there, touching me, kissing me, grounding me to the world and to them. I gave myself permission to lose control, to trust them to put me back together if I fell apart. I stopped fighting myself and rocked forward, then back. Fucking them. Making sure they understood that they were mine, that I wanted this. That this was *my choice*. Taking what they offered for myself, making both of my mates groan.

"You're mine. These cocks are mine." I squeezed them both, rocking back and forth on my hands and knees, milking them, pushing them, hoping they'd lose control.

Iavo shuddered, and Zach pulled me down for a kiss just as Iavo's hands wrapped around my hips and stopped me from moving.

Say yes, Brittany. Marry us. You haven't said yes.

I couldn't speak with Zach's tongue dueling with mine, so I tore my mouth from his. "I want you, but how can I marry two people? I don't understand."

Iavo slapped my ass, just hard enough for it to sting…and send a lightning bolt of shocked pleasure to my clit. My pussy fluttered, on the edge of orgasm, and my hands made fists in the bed sheets as Zach answered.

"You will marry me, Brittany. Iavo doesn't exist in the human world. According to human law, you'll be mine. But you're Dragonborn—"

I didn't let him finish. "Yes. You're mine. Both of you. Forever." Zach thrust up from beneath me, lifting his hips off the bed as Iavo thrust into me from behind, cutting off my words, my air. Again. I moaned and buried my face in Zach's shoulder, more than happy to hold on for the ride. But there was one more thing I needed to say, before things got completely wild. "And I'm not giving the ring back."

Zach chuckled, but his humor was short-lived as Iavo took control, fucking me harder and faster, rubbing his hard length against the thin layer separating him from Zach inside me.

We were both moaning as Iavo made his claim clear, commanding us to come when he did, his magic filling me, making my skin tingle, my clit burn, my entire body explode into a thousand little pieces.

I screamed as he slammed his body into me, as Zach shifted and fucked me, rubbing my clit. I was surrounded by heat and love and lust. And magic.

Iavo's seed, his magic, his essence filled me, the power pushing me right back over the edge for a second time as Zach filled me from below, the hard tip of his cock planting his seed in my womb, the dragon essence creating another Dragonborn child.

The knowledge filled me with a joy and peace I'd never

known. I wasn't worried about supporting a baby. For the first time in my life, I was content. Happy. For the first time, I knew I would never be alone again. Never have to fight the battle for survival on my own.

I was loved. Wanted. And the new life stirring inside me would be, too.

When it was over, they wrapped themselves around me in bed, the magic buzzing in the air making us all too lazy to move.

But Iavo couldn't resist. He pushed me onto my back and lay his head over my womb. *Hello, little one. I am your father, Iavo, The Protector, first of my name. And I will protect you. Always.*

Beside me, Zach watched with wide eyes. "You're kidding, right?"

I laughed and threw my arms around my new mates. So happy. My life was a miracle now. So wonderful I never could have imagined it. "No, he's not. I felt it happen."

"Boy or girl?"

I shrugged and looked at Iavo. His grin was worth a thousand years of suffering. *It matters not. The baby is mine.*

"Ours, Iavo. Ours. We need to work on expanding your vocabulary." Zach leaned in and kissed me, gently. "I love you, Brittany. But you're going to have to help me with this. Our dragon can be a bit hard to handle."

Javo, Queen's Lair, Mt. Rainier, Washington State

I HATED FLYING ALONE, but Zach and Brittany had been in the metal can of death as we raced to make it to the queen in time for Garrett's ceremony.

I had to fly high and fast, at altitudes that would kill my mate and my rider. So I'd flown above the jet, so high that I chased the stars.

The experience was soothing, and with my heart and soul firmly sealed with Brittany, I was truly at peace for the first time since I'd left the egg. That peace was gone now, as I led the way through the twisting tunnels of the queen's lair. I hadn't been home, really home, in a very long time, not since Zach and I were assigned to Arizona, to the canyons and the river lands that stretched from Colorado to Mexico. There had been no need to return to the cold, rainy northwest. Even when the queen summoned us for a mission, we were given our orders over the internet, or modern cell phones. It had been a long time since I'd been deep beneath the mountain, so deep the heat from Mother Earth's core pulsed and churned, lava beds long silent waiting to erupt heating the hot stones beneath our feet.

The pulse was like a living heartbeat, and it soothed me as little else could. It was the beating heart of my true mother, the Earth itself, radiating through the soles of my dragon feet as we walked to a place I thought never to see again.

To the hatching grounds.

What I saw filled me with despair.

The once pristine cave was run down, the shimmering magic in the walls—that only dragon eyes could see—faded from their once burning brightness to a faint flickering.

The queen was dying, and the hatching grounds barren. Less than a dozen eggs remained, and the few on the ground were larger than most. The eggs black or dark gray. The Night-breeds. Large, ferocious and difficult for a young rider to control, they were all that was left for Brittany's brother as we escorted him to the sacred ground.

The queen awaited us in her dragon form, stretched out across a massive throne made not from wood or metal but formed from the stones themselves with her own fiery breath. She looked beautiful, as always, the bright red dragon before us seemed to glow, her power pulsating with the heat of the rock beneath us. The magic flowing from her impossible to ignore or deny. Her orders to her sons were law, the magic flowing from her blood to ours impossible to disobey.

And I thanked whatever gods existed that my rider, Zach,

had been drawn to fire and not to ice. That my mother, the queen, was my master, and not my father. The king was ice to her fire. And he believed dragons should rule over man, as they had thousands of years ago. Humans were nothing to him but breeding females or slaves.

Like me, his sons could neither refuse him, nor disobey him, the pull of his magic too strong.

But perhaps his life, too, faded.

What that would mean for all of us, I had no idea, but that was not why we were here. Not today.

Today was meant for Garrett to join our ranks as a rider, to discover if a dragon would choose him, find him worthy.

Where are the rest of the eggs, Mother? I should have kept my mouth shut, but the question burned inside me like a wildfire, impossible to control.

Stolen, my son. I have sent other riders to find them and bring them back.

Stolen? By whom?

The large red dragon tilted her head to look at me as Zach turned on his heel, facing our queen. "When? Who took them? We will leave at once."

The queen shook her head. *No. The king sent his ice dragons to take them, to find riders more to his bidding.*

Zach looked as confused as I felt.

Why did they leave the Nightbreed eggs, Mother? They are the largest, the most powerful of our kind. I do not understand.

Brittany, who'd been holding both Zach's and Garrett's hands as they followed behind me, three humans under my protection, was the one who answered. I still forgot how lucky I was, that since we'd bonded completely, she could hear all dragons now, and their riders. She was truly mine. One of us. "Maybe whoever stole the eggs had a conscience. He couldn't disobey the king, but he left the most dangerous dragons behind. Out of his father's reach."

The queen's large head pivoted to inspect my mate and I felt Brittany's nervous energy through our new bond, stretched my wing just enough to shield most of her body from the queen's view.

Perhaps. The queen blinked, her ruby red lids sliding slowly over her giant eyes. *Where is my new rider? Bring him forward.*

Garrett, who'd spent the last two days coming to grips with his new reality, walked forward and knelt before the queen in the ancient ritual, as he'd been instructed to do by the others."

"My name is Garrett Anderson. I am Dragonborn. I claim the rights of a rider."

May one of my sons deem you worthy. Our queen inclined her terrifying head to the young human, who bravely held his ground. But then, he shared blood with my mate, and I knew her courage, her fearless nature, was one of the reasons I loved her.

Garrett bowed low to the queen and turned to the small stack of dragon eggs in the center of the cave floor. There were not many eggs. The brightly colored selection that had been scattered on the floor of the hatching chamber when Zach had come for me was gone.

Brittany was holding her breath, her fingers wrapped tightly over the top of my wing as I continued to shield her. I had never seen a Nightbreed born, and had no idea what a new hatchling might do. I would not allow even a moment of carelessness to put my mate in danger.

Normally, a rider would kneel and touch an egg he felt drawn to. The ritual was part magic and part instinct, two souls drawn to each other, complimenting one another to form a perfect pairing. I remember awakening in the egg, feeling the light of Zach's soul, the honor he possessed something I knew I would need to hold back my darker nature.

Garrett did not kneel, he stood, unmoving, staring at the largest egg in the center.

With a sound like wood breaking, the egg shattered as if it had exploded from the inside. In it's place stood a dragon with obsidian scales and glacier blue eyes. He was large, for a hatchling, the top of the dragon's head rising above Brittany's knees.

Brittany laughed, the sound of joy jolting all of us from our shock at the violent birth. "He's beautiful, brother."

Still on his feet, Garrett looked down at the dragon, their gazes locked. Held. The war of wills begun. The bonding of two souls. The moment when a dragon opened its mouth for the first time and breathed fire...or ice.

DID you enjoy Marked at Midnight? Read **Claiming His Mate...**

Octavia is enthralled by Prince Markus, yet outraged when the huge warrior takes her captive and informs her she is his fated mate.

Markus demands submission, and when the headstrong beauty questions his honor, he doles out sensual punishments that she likes more than she cares to admit, but can she forsake her people to stay by his side forever?

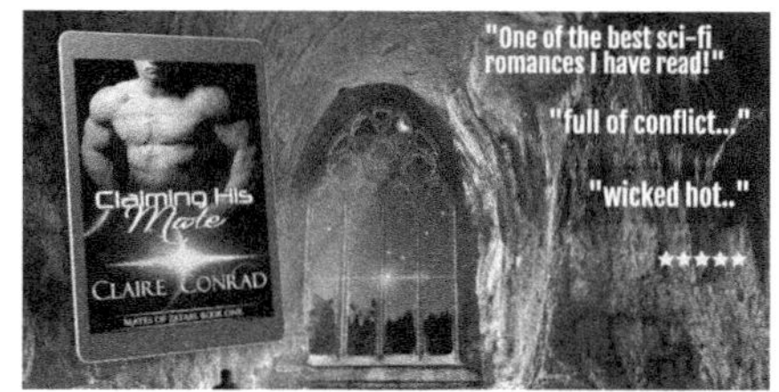
Claiming His
Mate
CLAIRE CONRAD
"One of the best sci-fi
romances I have read!"
"full of conflict..,"
"wicked hot.."

FIND OUT WHAT HAPPENS NEXT...

FIND OUT WHAT HAPPENS NEXT...

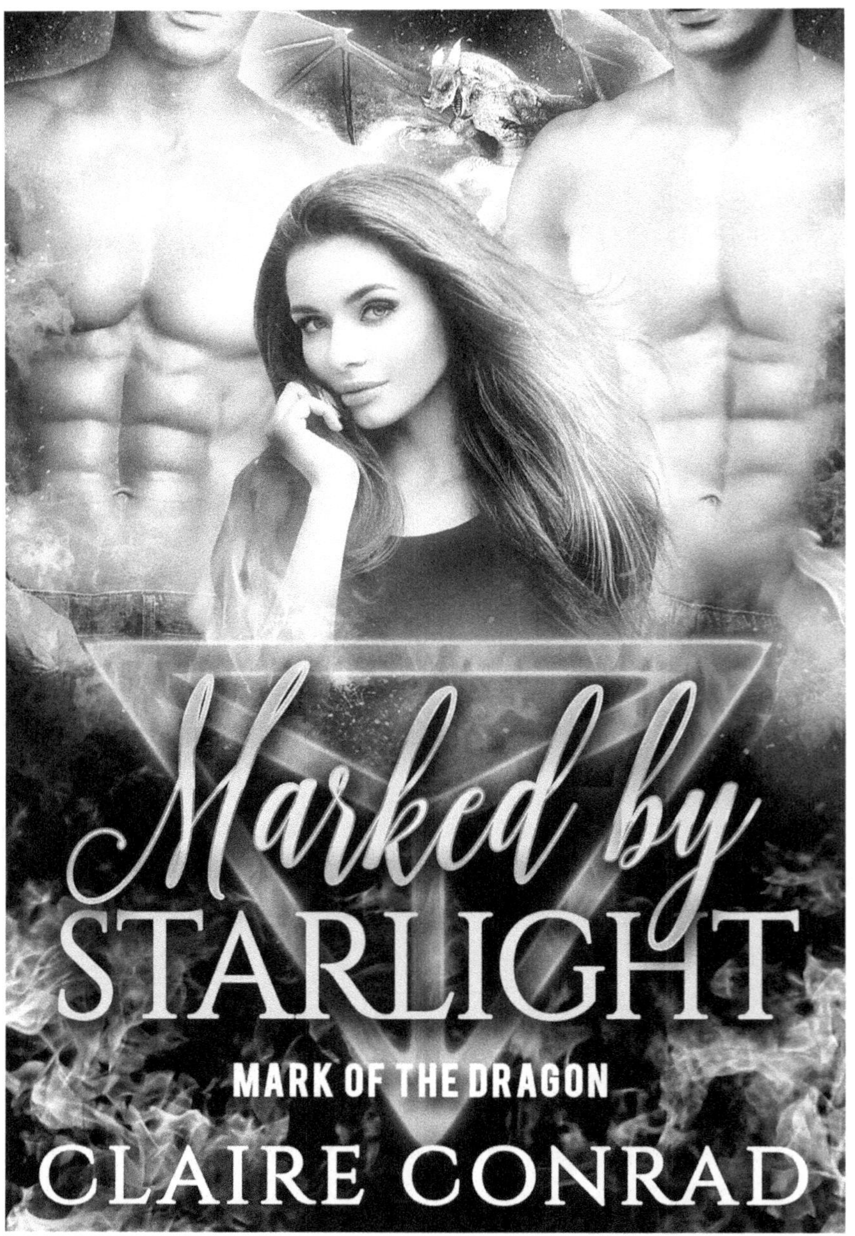

Visit www.ClaireCondrad.com for News and Alerts!

ABOUT THE AUTHOR

Join Claire's VIP Reader List HERE:
http://bit.ly/ClaireConrad

Claire Conrad is a full time writer and chocolate enthusiast who knows just enough about a handful of topics to dabble in many and master none. She loves a good red wine, traveling just about anywhere, coffee (as long as it's dark), romance and never met a sci-fi story she didn't love - including comically horrible "B" movies - much to her husband's chagrin. Claire writes sexy alpha males, aliens, shifters, undercover bad boys and anything else her muse thinks might be fun (or a little naughty).

www.ClaireConrad.com